SPIRIT OF THE SEA

Eleanor Jones

SPIRIT OF THE SEA

Copyright: Text © 2009 by Eleanor Jones
Cover and inside illustrations: Ketil Jakobsen Productions
Cover layout: Stabenfeldt AS

Typeset by Roberta L Melzl
Editor: Bobbie Chase
Printed in Germany, 2009

ISBN: 978-1-934983-39-3

Stabenfeldt, Inc.
225 Park Avenue South
New York, NY 10003
www.pony4kids.com

Available exclusively through PONY.

CHAPTER ONE

Sea, sky, and smooth untouched sand stretched out before them like a golden pathway beneath the awesome mass of the limestone cliffs. Waves crashed against the shore and rippled back into the incoming tide in froth of silvery foam. A single cloud, way, way up, scudded across the sky of clearest icy blue.

Grace Melrose felt as if she had lived her whole life for this perfect moment, mounted upon her own horse at last in the place that had totally overtaken her senses since she first came to live here just nine short months ago. Nine short months that felt like a lifetime, for it seemed to her now that her life hadn't really begun until she came to Beachy Heights – even though, initially, it was sadness that had brought her and her mother to the small white cottage on the cliff top.

She remembered that day now with a reluctant shiver. Her parents' break up had been hard for them both to bear – especially as her dad seemed to be so happy, but of course he had his new girlfriend. Over the last few months, though, it felt as if the ocean's soothing presence had helped to heal all that raw pain and anger. Now she was finally thinking forwards again and every day was filled with ideas and dreams, just as it was when she was very small. Had it done the same for her mother, she wondered with a sudden stab of guilt?

Her train of thought was short-lived, the momentary surge of guilt forgotten as Magic began to prance beneath her, champing eagerly on the bit, her silvery gray neck arched. The roar of the sea filled Grace's head. Her heart pounded in her ears. She gathered up the reins, all else forgotten as adrenalin flooded through her veins, overriding nerves and sidetracking common sense.

To gallop along this shore had been her dream, it seemed forever, a distant blurry vision that had only found reality in the last few months; a dream that had finally become possible for the first time ever in this very moment.

She shook her head, trying to stay grounded. Every sensible bone in her body told her that Magic, a high-strung four-year-old Thoroughbred, was far too wild still to cope with such excitement on her very first real outing. Still, the longing to just let her go was too strong to dismiss, even if it set their painstaking schooling back six months.

"Maybe just a canter, then, girl," she sighed, leaning forward to run a hand along the filly's curved crest and fixing her gaze through the sharply pointed ears ahead of her.

Way above them the awesome cliffs loomed, the cliffs that claimed so many desperate lives each year, lives that had gone wrong. *Now,* she suddenly realized, now was what really mattered. Live for today, for who knew what tomorrow might bring.

Softening her fingers on the reins she leaned forward, breathing the smell of the sea right down into her lungs. How had she survived before she came to this place? It may have taken heartbreak to bring her here but she knew that she would never ever leave it.

Magic snatched at the bit, eager to be off, and Grace half halted, trying to stifle the nerves that brought back common sense. What if she couldn't stop; what if the newly broken filly totally forgot her training in all the excitement?

The strip of glistening sand stretched out before her. The salty tang of sea air caressed her skin.

"Live for today," she breathed, closing her calves around Magic's heaving sides. The silver gray horse needed no further encouragement. She leaped forward, tossing her beautiful head, snorting in rhythm with her stride as she increased her pace. And then there was nothing but the sheer elation of speed. The pounding of hooves on the smooth, firm surface, bulging muscles, straining sinews, strands of silvery mane lashing her face.

Grace kept a firm hold on the reins, concentrating the filly's attention on what lay ahead. Never had she known such a sense of power and speed, the exhilaration of being totally at one with another living creature. This must be how it felt to ride in a race, but no, this had to be so much better, for this was just she and her horse, two beings molded together in perfect empathy.

The moment when that empathy disappeared came suddenly. It flashed by in a moment and yet lasted a lifetime. Glancing down for a second she saw something, below them on the sand. Hoof prints! Hoof prints leading into the sea... but how?

That one momentary lapse of concentration was all it took. Magic spooked, leaping sideways as if some invisible monster had risen from the ocean and whirled around to face the horizon, head held high and nostrils flaring.

Grace clung to her mane, desperately holding on with her legs as she was flung to one side. The sand beneath them loomed, but all she could think of was her precious horse, loose on the huge expanse of beach, free to gallop off wherever she chose.

For what seemed an eternity she hung on grimly, halfway between safety and the sand below. Sheer determination dragged her slowly back upright, and then suddenly Magic seemed to loom up beneath her, spinning away from the crashing waves. She reared with a piercing whinny, flailing the air with her hooves, and Grace was lost. The ground came to meet her, solid and painful, but the pain in her heart hurt far more, for the pale gray filly was already galloping, head up and tail flowing like a silver banner behind her... back toward home and the busy road to Brighton.

Grace clambered to her feet in a painful daze, seeing the hoof prints again through a distant blur. They were heading into the sea, but how...? Her eyes fell upon the other set of hoof prints that lead off along the shoreline, Magic's hoof prints.

Automatically she started to follow them, running awkwardly, desolation overriding the ache that clawed at

her back. But what was the point? Magic was almost out of sight already. She stopped in her tracks, desperately looking around; there had to be a better way.

Above her a lazy curl of smoke rose into the clear blue sky, the smoke from Sea View cottage, *their* cottage. It was just up there on the very top of the cliffs, so near and yet so far away. If there had only been a way to get up the cliff face she could have cut Magic off before she got home, or maybe even stopped her before she came to Brighton Road. At least then her mother would never know about her fall. Even if the horse did manage to survive the gallop home, Grace was sure that Sue Melrose would say that she had to go; Magic was only just being tolerated as it was.

Her mother had been furious when she and her father came back from the sale with a half-broken and very nervous four-year-old, but Todd Melrose had been unable to resist his daughter's pleas to buy the beautiful Thoroughbred; this horse was *his* gift, his way to appease the guilt he felt for hurting his family so. Sue, however, had only begrudgingly agreed to let Grace give horse ownership a try in the first place, and he had promised to buy her a sensible first horse, something sturdy, reliable and super safe... everything Magic wasn't.

Horrified by the prospect of her fifteen-year-old daughter taking on the wild looking youngster, she had tried to make him take the horse back to the dealer right there and then.

It was Grace who managed to win her mother over. "At least give me a chance to *try* and train her," she had pleaded. "She looks so scared... and I promise to send her back at the first hint of trouble."

Her stomach churned now as she remembered that promise. This was definitely trouble with a capital T and maybe… a lump of emotion choked her throat as she imagined the worst scenario. Maybe after today there would be no Magic to send back anyway.

A vision of a life without the horse she had grown to love so much loomed desolately before her. Oh, if only she had remembered to bring her cell phone, at least then she could have called someone for help, but she had been so exited to be actually riding her own horse for the very first time that everything else had slipped her mind…

She remembered her mother's pale, worried face that morning as she dashed off for her important interview. *"Don't go further than the end of the lane and don't forget your phone,"* were her final instructions, instructions that had gone completely out of Grace's head as soon as she put her foot in the stirrup.

Hope faded. It was too late already, and her mother was sure to be home by now… sure to see Magic come galloping rider-less along the lane… but what if? A crazy idea filtered through the panic that was messing with her head. What if she *could* somehow find a way to get up the cliffs?

Grace stopped, her heart thumping hard against the wall of her chest as fear and excitement jostled for first place. She about-turned, desperately scouring the cliff face. Crumbling white rock loomed ahead of her, an impossible barrier… or was it? Her clear gray eyes fell upon the pathway that had been used long ago by visitors to Beachy Heights, until the force of the sea eventually undercut the rock face, making the route unsafe. There were still parts of the metal railings left, showing where the path had once been. The bottom of it was securely fenced off and a sign had been placed there… "DANGER." The word jumped out at her, making her stomach churn. This was crazy; it was impossible to climb up there. *But life without Magic is impossible too,* whispered an inner voice. With a surge of determination, she set off at a jog trot toward the towering cliffs, forcing herself to focus. She had to try to do this, for there was no other way.

At first it was easy to lend false confidence. Her hands fixed themselves firmly onto the jagged rocks; her feet found purchase where the pathway was worn smooth by so many long gone feet. Below her the sea raged and she glanced down, disconcerted. The tide was coming in; she *had* to go now. The rail beneath her fingers wobbled and she moved her hand quickly back to the rock, fighting off her fear with images of Magic, safe in the stone stable behind the cottage with its back to the wind that howled constantly over the cliff top. She refused to allow the other images into her mind, images of the filly's pale shape, broken and bleeding, the red blood sharply contrasting her silvery coat. She had to do this for her horse's sake; there was no going back.

Even where the railings had disappeared into the sea below she could still see parts of the pathway. It was going to be OK, she was sure of it.

Inching her way upward she clung to the rock face like a leech, the pain in her fingers making her forget the fiery ache in her back. How long had she been climbing, and where would Magic be now? Maybe she was home already, maybe her mother was setting out to look for her right now. Oh, how she longed for the comfort and security of Sea View Cottage. Oh, how she wished that she had never started this crazy climb in the first place.

The endless stretch of sky above darkened, its brilliant clear blue giving way to rolling gray clouds. Even the weather was turning against her. A sob rose in her throat and she took a breath, stopping for a moment to press her face against the cold, harsh rock.

"I can do this," she whispered into the moaning wind as the first waves covered the sand and crept to the base of the cliff. She climbed on valiantly, not daring to look down, trying to close her ears to the sound of the breakers crashing onto the rocks below… Cutting off any hope of going back the way she came.

Just when she thought that she was going to have to let go, to end her struggle to survive – for it had gone far beyond just trying to save Magic… now she was also trying to save herself – the pathway widened, as if some kind hand had reached out to help her. Crazy images flashed into her mind; maybe this pathway was haunted, maybe one of those ancient peoples really was holding out a hand to her. Strangely, the idea was comforting and she paused for a moment, concentrating on breathing before valiantly climbing on.

Steeling herself to look upwards, she found a niche with her toe and reached for a piece of railing that hung above her. One big effort, and then the path widened… if she could just… She stretched out her arm; her fingers wrapped themselves around the cold metal… One big pull and…

13

As the railing came away in her hand she felt a sense of disbelief. No fear… No panic… just an awesome sense of loss. Now she was never going to be able to help Magic. Never going to be able to finish her training… never going to…

The sound of the sea was inside her head, filling her mind. Waves crashed against the rocks below and the wind howled, calling her home. She fell silently, her arms flailing as she reached out desperately for the mystical helping hand. For a moment she thought she felt ghostly fingers winding themselves around her hand, but then the sea came up to meet her, cold and dark and deep, taking away her breath… her life… her future.

CHAPTER TWO

So was this death? As the water closed over Grace's head the question flashed into her mind, its answer inevitable. It couldn't be death, for she had to save Magic; she couldn't die yet, for she had so much to do. Anyway, somehow she had missed the rocks on the way down so that must be a sign. This was water, just water; all she had to do was swim.

The will to survive strengthened her. She thrust herself upwards toward the light, images whirling around inside her head, images of her mother and her father, holding out their arms, images of Magic's beautiful head raised in greeting. Images that spun and spun until they formed into one shapeless mass. Every bone in her body ached and her lungs burned inside her chest, weakening her resolve as the sea took her in its mighty grip, tossing her this way and that, like a toy in the very jaws of death, playing with her puny life. She was in another place now, beyond fear, beyond panic, beyond any lucid thought except to live, and it seemed that even that was not enough. As she found her way to the surface, taking in a gulp of precious air, the force of the water thrust her helplessly toward the cruel rocks that pulled her down and down and down… into the darkness.

Grace was oblivious at first to the force that thrust her upwards, until light burst back into her world, oblivious to the return of life until oxygen flooded her lungs. And then came another kind of pain, the pain of disbelief, for this had to be just a crazy dream.

Beneath her she felt the solid power of muscle and sinew, bearing her up, carrying her, half-conscious, through the crashing waves. She rode the sea in her dreams and in her memories, mounted upon a great gray horse that galloped toward the safety of the shore. Mighty hooves thundering soundlessly through the seething ocean, long strands of mane lashing her face as she clung to the great arch of crest before her. Could this be real?

And then, somehow, her fingers were clawing at the sand, feeling its firm softness. *It* was real; it had to be… but how? The light hurt her eyes and she rolled away from it, clambering to her knees, lowering her eyelids trying to focus her blurred vision. Way over to her left was the cliff she had tried to climb. She blinked, unable to concentrate on reality. How had she gotten here? Memories of an invisible horse flooded her mind and crazy sensations brought a quiver to her very core. She sank back onto the sand. No, this was madness, there had to be another explanation.

A huge gull loomed into her view, settling down nearby, staring at her through bright, unblinking eyes.

Did it know? Had the gull seen the powerful, magical, unbelievable force that brought her safely through the crashing waves? It flapped its broad wings and let out a lonely cry, rising slowly into the rolling gray sky. No matter, the force that saved her was not the question; she would dwell on it later. She was alive and that, along with saving Magic, were all that really mattered.

As she stumbled to her feet her whole body ached with a pain so fierce that she fell back onto the sand, gasping for breath, her blurred eyes falling upon imprints in its smooth, golden surface. Hoof prints…? Were they Magic's hoof prints? No! She shook her head, trying to clear it. The hoof prints came out of the sea and… she traced one with her finger. They were unshod prints, leading up the shore and back again… into the sea. Memories flooded her mind again, awesome physical impressions of a powerful horse, lifting her through the mighty waves, carrying her to safety. She struggled to her feet. This was madness, her imagination going crazy, it had to be. She must think forward… must get home. Must…? Magic, she had to find Magic.

Shivering in the blustery wind she set off along the shoreline, trying to ignore the waves of dizziness and pain that clouded her vision. Her wet clothes clung to her and her feet squelched inside her boots, but she forced herself to keep walking, concentrating on the cluster of cottages on the horizon. Magic might be up there. Maybe someone had caught her, or maybe she had just stopped to graze somewhere… Maybe she was already lying on the busy Brighton Road… Maybe there were people there too, killed by Grace's negligence.

Hope died, filtering away with her dreams. Maybe her life was over. Maybe she should have perished in the sea when she fell from the cliff. Maybe she should never have been born. After all, it was she who had introduced her father to Tina, the girl who had changed their whole lives; everything was her fault. Regret was a weight too heavy to bear, and for a moment she stopped in her tracks. Perhaps she should just run away…

But no, she shook her head. What was she thinking? Magic, Heathwaite Magical Mist, the horse she had dreamed of for all of her life, was probably home already waiting for her. Fighting off all the negative thoughts, she broke onto a run. It wasn't too late, she knew it with a certainty that slowed her heartbeat and brought new purpose to her stride.

At the bottom of the pathway that led up from the shore toward the cluster of low roofed cottages, she stopped for a moment, holding her side. Was that a whinny? The pain in her lungs forgotten, she forced her weary legs up the steep slope and out onto the headland. Way behind her the sea stretched toward the horizon, a shimmering mass, and ahead of her the coarse grass of the cliff top rose in a mound beyond the cottages. Around the edge of it ran the lane that meandered toward Brighton Road. Had Magic galloped along there, or had she wanted to feel the grass beneath her hooves? Or maybe she had become completely disorientated and gone the opposite way altogether… toward the town.

"You all right, dear?"

The friendly voice from just behind her made her jump.

She stopped in her tracks, looking around to see a small elderly woman staring at her with bright, twinkling eyes.

"You've had a fall." It was a statement, not a question, but Grace nodded.

"The sea… I … I fell in the sea. Have you seen my horse?"

"My grandson would like a horse like that," the woman responded.

"You've seen her?" gasped Grace. "Where is she?" And then came the whinny again, above the sound of the buffeting wind, distinctive and close at hand.

"I shut the gate," said the woman proudly, beckoning her to follow. "It wouldn't do for her to get onto Brighton Road, would it? My name is Mollie, by the way, Mollie Jenkins."

"I'm Grace," she responded, willing the old lady to walk a bit faster. Mollie leaned on her arm for support, limping slightly and breathing heavily.

"My old joints don't seem to work like they once did," she laughed. "I used to ride too, when I was your age. You'd never believe it now. Come on, she's just along here."

Grace's heart turned over as Mollie pointed toward a wooded area of crooked, stunted trees behind the row of cottages. Could it really be Magic the old lady had seen? Could she really be that lucky? Maybe it was a totally different horse altogether.

The leafless trees leaned toward the ground in unison, forced to grow sideways by the constant buffeting of the ceaseless wind that swept over the cliff top. Grace scoured their dark shapes for a glimpse of silvery white, to no avail.

"Where, though… *where* is she, and is she all right?"

she cried out as they went through the narrow rickety gate that led into a small paddock. "...Is she hurt?"

Mollie's gray head swung from side to side. "Not as I noticed, but she would have been if I hadn't shut the gate."

"But what gate...? Surely she didn't go through here."

"See for yourself," said Mollie proudly.

Magic stood close to the trees, around the other side of them, her tail to the blustery wind. She still wore her tack, but her broken reins were trailing on the ground and dark streaks of sweat marked her silver coat. She looked up with a start when she saw the two people approach, spinning around to face them, her pointed ears pricked so sharply forward that they seemed almost to touch at their tips.

Relief flooded over Grace, leaving her shaking. "Magic," she cried out, rushing toward her. The nervous filly snorted, and Grace pulled a piece of carrot from her sodden pocket.

"Steady, girl... steady... it's all right now." The filly lowered her beautiful head, blowing through her nostrils before gently taking the carrot from the palm of her girl's hand.

"You see," remarked Mollie, folding her arms across her chest. "I told you she was fine."

"Yes..." Grace's dark eyes shone with gratitude. "Thank you. You don't know how much this means to me."

The old lady's bright eyes twinkled in response. "Oh, I think I do," she smiled. "Now you had better get home to dry yourself out. You'll catch your death of cold if you don't get out of those wet clothes."

"Catch your death... catch your death... catch your death..." Those three words whirled around inside Grace's

20

head. She almost *had* caught her death, but it wasn't from the cold. Oh, how much she longed to be home in the cozy cottage on the cliff top with Magic safely rugged up in her stable... If it hadn't been for Mollie...

"Will I see you again...?" she began, wanting to let the old lady know just how grateful she was, but when she looked around Mollie was already walking slowly off down the lane.

"Goodbye," she called, "and thanks." Her voice disappeared, whisked away on the blustery wind, and she turned her attention back to Magic. She would come back here again soon, she decided; maybe even buy her a small present... After all, she must live somewhere close by.

It was no small job to tie the broken reins, and after a quick inspection of each fragile-looking limb, Grace picked them up and looked around for the quickest way home. Could Magic really have come through that narrow gate? No, of course not. There was another larger one further up, just on the side of the lane. Magic must have seen it open when she came galloping around the corner and gone into the paddock. Thank heaven Mollie just happened to be there to shut it behind her.

"You will never be so lucky again," she told the subdued looking horse as it followed willingly behind her. Magic tossed her head as if in understanding, and Grace stopped for a second to give her a pat.

"All's well that ends well, I suppose," she smiled, shivering slightly. Suddenly she was very aware of her clinging wet clothing.

"Come on..."

Fastening the gate behind them, she placed her toe

into the stirrup and swung up into the saddle, staring at the world through her horse's pricked ears as though it was the most wonderful sight she had ever seen. After all, on more than one occasion this afternoon she had believed it to be a view that she would never see again.

"Let's go home," she sighed.

The relief at finding Magic so easily, safe and unhurt, was replaced by apprehension as they approached Sea View Cottage. She hadn't quite gotten away with it yet, for her mother was sure to notice her wet clothing, and if she started asking questions Grace knew that she wouldn't be able to lie. Anyway, she *wanted* to tell someone, *wanted* to let out all the pent-up emotion. But who would believe her? Who would believe that she fell down a cliff and was saved from certain drowning by an invisible force, a force that felt in every way like a huge, powerful horse? No, it was madness. She shivered, suddenly unable to stop her teeth from chattering, but how was she going to keep such an awesome secret?

Magic was her first priority. Trying to put the terrifying events of the afternoon in the back of her mind and focus on now, she slipped down from the saddle on shaking legs. Her mother's small blue car was not in the driveway, so maybe she had a reprieve after all; this could be the luckiest day of her life.

"Or unluckiest, if you think about it another way," she said out loud to Magic, who tossed her head and snorted, eager for her feed. "Think positive, that's the thing," decided Grace, unbuckling the girth. "So I think I'll go for luckiest."

Twenty minutes later the gray filly was happily

tucking into her hay net, knee deep in fresh straw and warmly rugged in the new mauve checked blanket that Todd Melrose had brought over just yesterday. Grace had been going to keep it for a special occasion but this, she decided, was probably one of the most special occasions she would ever have; the outcome could have been so different that it didn't bear thinking about.

"All's well that ends well, girl," she said, giving Magic one final pat before heading eagerly for the cottage. The driveway was still empty, she noted, and her heart lifted; maybe her mother would never need to know about the day's adventure after all.

The shudder that ran through her as memories flooded in spoke of far more than the cold. She had to tell someone, though, for how could she keep such an awesome experience to herself? Then again, who would believe her?

She fumbled beneath the stone for the back door key and turned it in the lock, opening the solid oak door and slipping into their warm, cozy kitchen with a sigh of relief. She was home; warm pine cupboards, brown and white checked tablecloth, everything familiar and so wonderfully ordinary. A note fluttered on the table, held down by the small pink pig that her mother bought last week at a charity shop; Sue Melrose collected pigs.

Had to skip into town, hon. Back in an hour.
Please put a log on the fire.
Mom xxx

Grace picked it up and read it through twice, suddenly consumed by an awesome sense of loneliness. Then she opened the door of the wood-burning stove with a heartfelt sigh, clinging to its warmth for a moment before throwing on one of the logs from the basket beside the hearth. Sparks spluttered from it and she quickly closed the door again. A bath, that's what she needed; a long, hot soak to ease her aching muscles.

She was still in the bath half an hour later when Sue Melrose came running up the stairs.

"Had a successful day, hon?" she called from the landing. Grace slipped down deeper into the warm, comforting water.

"Kind of," she responded.

Her mother's smiling face appeared around the door. "Only kind of?"

"Well, I suppose in a way you could say that it was very successful," she admitted, thinking of how tragic it might have been.

"Well that's good then. So have I. I'll tell you all about it over dinner and then we'll watch that new series on TV."

Suddenly, to Grace, it seemed like the best idea anyone had ever had.

"I'll be down in a minute," she called as her mother's footsteps disappeared down the stairs. She was home, and that was all that mattered. Now she just had to try and move on, forget the whole terrifying experience… if that was possible.

CHAPTER THREE

Grace was sure that she would be unable to sleep a wink after her traumatic day. She snuggled down beneath her comforter and closed her eyes, trying to think of anything but her crazy climb and... No! She forced her thoughts away from the images that flashed into her head, trying to settle her mind on something else; the magical day when she and her dad had gone to the Wigton horse sale, for instance.

Of course, he hadn't intended to buy a horse like Magic – he'd been going for an elderly, safe plodder – but the gray filly had just been so... so... She rolled over, pulling her comforter up close around her chin, remembering that beautiful head, those huge, frightened dark eyes looking right at her, pleading for help.

She had plucked urgently at her father's sleeve. "That's the one... look. Can we bid on her?"

Todd Melrose had laughed, she remembered, a great guffaw that made everyone look around. "I don't think

so," he had smiled, ruffling her dark bangs. "You know what I promised your mother… If you have to have a horse then it must be something safe and reliable, and that, definitely, is neither."

Grace had straightened her hair with her fingers, disappointment clawing at her stomach as she flicked through the catalogue looking for the horse's number.

611. Heathwaite Magical Mist. Gray Thoroughbred filly. Four years old. Lightly backed in spring and turned away. Sold sound with no vices.

Totally *unsuitable* as a first horse, to be honest, but what did suitability have to do with it? She wanted a horse she could keep for all of its life, so maybe the filly was suitable after all. They could grow old together.

She had told that to her father, who had merely laughed and kept on scouring his catalogue for sleepy-looking hairy cobs with kind eyes and sad faces.

At twelve o'clock he declared that they would take a lunch break and disappeared to get them both a sandwich and a drink from the stall near the entrance while Grace *supposedly* inspected a plump piebald gelding. Seizing her opportunity and drawn like metal to a magnet, she had raced back to speak to the small elderly man who held Magic's lead rope.

"She's a real lady," he told her. "Bred to race. Needs a little understanding, that's all… She'll be a star one day."

"Star one day… star one day… star one day." The words rang around in Grace's head as she curled up into a fetal position, cuddling her pillow. One thing was for sure; Magic certainly hadn't shown any stardom yesterday; quite the reverse, in fact. Maybe her mother

was right. Perhaps she *was* totally unsuitable for a fifteen-year-old girl to train. No…! With every fiber of her being Grace rejected the idea. Magic was her soul mate, no matter what anyone said. She had known it the first time she saw her, and she was sure of it still.

The old man had fumbled in his pocket, she remembered, eager for a sale, pulling out some crumpled papers. When the nervous youngster snorted, jumping back, he yanked on her head collar and Grace had just longed to press her cheek against the silvery softness of her nose and tell her that everything was going to be OK… Just like it was going to be OK now, she realized with fresh determination. They could get through this; she knew it. And anyway, no matter what, nothing would ever make her regret that day.

"This is her breeding," the man had announced, thrusting the papers at her. "There's some good blood in there. She's only four years old, of course, but if someone spends a bit of time with her, they'll have a winner."

"Grace!!" Her father's voice had made her jump, and she had looked around guiltily to see him holding two cups.

"But Dad…" she had pleaded.

"You'd do well buying the girl something worthwhile, you know," the old man had nodded, winking at Grace. "This filly could be worth a fortune one day. All she needs is a little love."

"I could do it, Dad… I know I could. I'd spend hours with her." Still, her father had not been persuaded. A fat black cob had gone under the hammer and he had put in a reluctant bid; to Grace's relief, it had gone for more than he had wanted to pay. Then had come a scrawny bay that was supposedly an ideal first horse. She had held her breath when it had kicked out at its handler just as her father had been about to raise his hand… The gray filly had been next, and her heart had felt as if it might burst.

"Please… please… please, Dad," she had cried, clinging to his arm. The price had gone up and stuck… it seemed that quiet first ponies were far more desirable that wild-looking Thoroughbreds. Grace had stood up, catching the auctioneer's quick eye. "Come on, pal," he had shouted with glee, looking at her father. "Give the little lady a treat. Just think what a picture they'd make together."

A ripple of approval had run through the gathered crowd and all eyes had turned toward them, as if daring Todd to bid. Tears had welled up in Grace's clear gray eyes as the auctioneer tried again.

"You'll never get another bargain like it," he yelled. Her father had raised his hand so slowly that at first she hadn't even noticed it.

"Going once…"

She had begun to shiver.

"Going twice…"

She had felt sick.

"Gone!!!" The plump, bald auctioneer had called with glee. "Sold to…?" "Melrose," her father had croaked. "Todd Melrose."

That magical moment was the last thing in Grace's head until, unbelievably, she woke with a start to the sound of her mother's voice. Could it really be morning? Could she really have actually slept after yesterday? Unwanted memories flooded in.

"Grace!" called her mother again. "Grace, Your father is here to pick you up. Come on, you haven't even done Magic yet. What's wrong with you this morning?"

"Yes, lazy bones," joined in Todd Melrose. "I'll go and start mucking out while your mother puts some bacon on."

For a moment, Grace felt totally disorientated. To hear her mother and father together was just like old times. Had she missed something here? She scrambled out of bed, deliberately trying *not* to think about yesterday and wondering how she had managed to sleep so soundly.

She walked into the kitchen, still fastening her shirt. The aroma of bacon assaulted her nostrils and hunger pangs took over.

"Did I really hear Dad saying that he was going to muck out?" she asked with disbelief.

Sue Melrose looked up from the stove. "Incredibly, yes," she replied, going back to tend the sizzling pan.

"Well, I'd better go and help him."

"If I were you I would eat your breakfast and leave him to it," remarked Sue in caustic tone.

Grace sighed. So things hadn't really changed after all. "I'll just have a bacon sandwich then, please," she announced. "So that I can take it with me."

Before her mother could reply, Todd appeared in the doorway. He ran one hand through his mop of dark hair and grinned.

"Done," he exclaimed with pride.

"Ah, but how well done, Dad?" responded Grace.

"Badly, I imagine," retorted her mother.

"Actually," his handsome face glowed with pride. "Actually, I think I've done pretty well."

31

Sue sniffed, but Grace ignored her.

"So you've mucked out already *and* fed Magic?" Grace asked with a smile.

"Well, something like that," he admitted. "You had better go and check on her, though… after we've eaten your mother's delicious breakfast, of course."

Sue scowled at him, but Grace could see the delight in her eyes at his comments.

"Well, I've had mine, but you and Mom have yours together," she suggested.

"I have to go out now," remarked Sue curtly. "And I'm sure that your father can find much better company than mine… Oh, and by the way, where *is* Tina this morning, Todd?"

Grace was surprised to see her father squirm.

"She was called into work," he told them, too quickly. "Come on, Grace, we'd better get going."

"But what about breakfast?"

He held his wife's gaze and sat down abruptly. "Right… well… OK, thanks, I am pretty hungry, so it happens."

Sue could not help a wry smile. "Oh, so she didn't make you breakfast before she left?"

"I'm going to check on Magic and put her out into the paddock," sighed Grace. "You two are like a couple of kids."

As she left the kitchen she heard a burst of laughter and smiled to herself. Maybe it wasn't too late for her parents after all.

Todd Melrose had promised to buy Grace a new bridle for Magic and as his low-slung, sporty car zoomed along the highway toward Field House saddlers, she found herself trying to find the right moment to tell him about yesterday. She couldn't tell her mother for fear of losing Magic, but maybe he would understand. It just felt like such an awesome burden to bear on her own. Maybe if it had been school time she could have told Nell, her new school friend – well, the only school friend she had made since moving to Newbury High, to be honest. She imagined the scenario now.

"Oh and by the way, I went out riding on the beach yesterday, and my horse spooked and threw me, so I tried to climb up the rock face and fell into the sea. But guess what? I would have definitely drowned if a great invisible horse type thing hadn't come up underneath me and carried me to the shore. I know it was real because I saw his hoof prints…"

No, she realized, she couldn't tell Nell because then she probably wouldn't even *be* her friend anymore… In fact, Nell might tell the rest of the class, and she would be branded as some kind of weird freak who made up stories and was laughed at by everyone.

Her father's voice broke her train of thought. "Things aren't too good between Tina and me, I'm afraid," he remarked sadly.

Grace's heart fell; there went her last chance to unburden the memories that were driving her crazy. She stared out of the window, watching the blur of scenery flash by, wanting to say, "I told you so," but listening anyway.

"Just go back to Mom," she suggested when he finally fell silent.

"We'll see," he smiled. "Sorry about that, love. Come on, let's talk about you."

Grace shrugged, searching for the right words to make him believe her story.

"I took Magic on the shore for the first time yesterday…" she tentatively began.

"Oh look, we're here already," he exclaimed as the sign for the saddlers loomed up ahead of them. "Now what was it we're getting?"

Stifling her feelings with a deep sigh, Grace tried to summon some enthusiasm. She had wanted a new bridle for ages but now, suddenly, it didn't seem quite so important.

He parked the car and cut the engine, catching her eye as he reached for his jacket.

"Sorry love, what were you going to tell me?"

"Nothing," she shrugged. "Nothing important… and it's a bridle, by the way. You said that you would buy me a new bridle, remember? For when we start going to shows."

"Shows, huh?" he smiled. "Magic must be doing well, then. We proved your mother wrong, didn't we, love? I knew you could do it."

Grace squirmed inside. She *couldn't* do it, could she? How could she tell her father the truth now? How could she dampen the pride that shone in his eyes? The answer came quickly; she couldn't. She would just have to try a bit harder, that was all, and put yesterday behind her.

CHAPTER FOUR

It was one thing to *decide* to put her terrifying experience behind her and another to actually manage to do it, Grace realized. Over the next few weeks she spent hours in the paddock behind the cottage, perfecting Magic's schooling. Maybe if she taught her to be obedient enough, when they next ventured onto the shore – as she knew one day they must – then the filly's training would override her excitement, or at least that was the plan. She tried not to think about the great horse that carried her to safety, preferring to believe that it was simply a product of her semi-conscious, half drowned state of mind. She was just lucky, she told herself, lucky to have been washed up on the shore.

As she made another endless circle, half-halting before she asked for walk, Grace realized that the time had come. Magic was behaving like an angel, the sun was high in the sky and even the wind had dropped for once.

"Just do it," she told herself, leaning forwards onto the filly's neck.

"Will you promise to behave yourself, girl?"

"I'm going now, hon," called her mother's voice from over by the cottage. "I'll be back about five."

Grace lifted her arm in farewell before going straight into a balanced canter, absorbing the smooth rhythm of Magic's stride with her seat. Her mother had been so much more relaxed since starting her new job that she didn't even give her a hard time about being careful anymore, so she wouldn't object. And her father…
Her heart fell. Her father thought that she was going to compete in the local riding club spring show next month. He was so proud of her; how could she tell him that she didn't even dare to go out on a trail ride?

That final thought decided her actions. Taking a deep breath, she turned Magic's nose toward the gate. She had always prided herself on being brave, and she wasn't going to let this get to her any more…

"Now or never," she whispered. Just to the top of the pathway down to the shore would do for today, and maybe she would meet the old lady who had saved Magic. What was her name? Mollie, that was it, Mollie Jenkins. It was time she said "thank you," anyway.

Once decided, Grace began really to enjoy her ride along the narrow lane. The whole world was bursting with new life, and she breathed in the fresh spring air with a sense of joy. She had put her experience behind her, she was sure of it; maybe they could go to the riding club spring show after all. Maybe her dad would build her some jumps in the paddock. Her mind began to swirl with possibilities.

Even Brighton Road was quiet for once. As Magic trotted obediently across it, her hooves ringing out on the smooth new surface, Grace could see the sea ahead of her, smooth today and glistening, hiding its rage.

"I don't know, girl. What was I thinking?" she said. Magic tossed her beautiful head as if in response, whinnying gently and staring into the distance.

"You see," she went on determinedly, as they approached the top of the pathway that led down to the long golden sweep of the shore. "It really is perfectly harmless."

To the left of them were the cottages where the old lady lived and there was the paddock where… Something inside her tightened. Perhaps it was time to go back. Magic pulled at the reins, her whole body tense with excitement, and Grace circled her away.

"Not today, girl," she said in a firm tone. "Come on. We need to get home and do some practicing."

For a moment the filly balked, whinnying loudly, but Grace nudged her firmly forward, back toward home. When Magic gave in obediently her heart swelled with pride; all that training really had paid off. She breathed in the salty air, looking toward the wide blue sky that stretched toward the distant horizon, beyond the shimmering sea, and for just a moment she found herself searching for a glimpse of a mighty horse leaping through the waves. Shuddering, she looked determinedly away, urging Magic into a brisk trot. It was total nonsense; she knew that, just her crazy imagination running away with her.

They were halfway home when Magic suddenly

stopped dead, snorting loudly, at the place where the lane passed close to the edge of the cliff. Grace fell forward onto her neck, taken totally by surprise.

"What is it, girl? What did you see?"

The gray filly stood like a rock, ears sharply pricked, staring toward the horizon, and screamed a defiant whinny toward the rolling waves way, way below them.

The high-pitched sound made Grace's head ring. "Stop it," she cried, reaching down to slap her neck. When Magic ignored her she turned her around in a circle and kicked her firmly forwards. The filly gave in begrudgingly, and although for the next half-mile or so she pranced and sidled, Grace's determination overcame any nerves she may have felt. By the time Sea View cottage came into sight she had Magic back under full control again.

"There, you see," she exclaimed out loud, heaving a sigh of relief. "Home again, safe and sound."

She didn't see Magic's dark shining eyes roll back in the direction of the sea, didn't notice the shudder of anticipation that rippled through her body as her sharply pricked ears caught a distant, muffled sound.

Someone else did, though. An interested observer with dark, twinkling eyes, who had watched in admiration as Grace skillfully controlled the nervous filly on the cliff top. He stood now on the slope behind the cottage, wondering whether or not to make his presence known. He saw Magic staring out to sea and a shudder of apprehension ran down his spine as it suddenly dawned on him just why she looked so familiar.

Confusion flooded his mind and he turned away, calling softly to the huge Irish Wolf hound that lay at his feet.

"Come on, boy, let's go home."

Grace looked up and noticed him just as he moved away. Who was he, the tall teenage boy with the big gray dog at his heels? She had never seen him at school, or was he older than that? Magic nudged her, eager for her feed, and she laughed.

"OK girl, don't worry, it's coming."

When she looked up again the boy and dog were gone; she slotted them into her memory and focused on the present.

Twenty minutes later when Magic was brushed off, rugged up and happily plunging her nose into a bucket of mix, chop and sugar beet, Grace hitched her saddle onto her hip and slung her bridle over one shoulder. Its reins trailed unnoticed on the floor as she closed the stable door and headed toward the cottage.

"I hope that's not the new one," warned her father, suddenly appearing from behind the high gray stone wall that helped to shield the small stable yard from the ceaseless wind.

"Of course not," retorted Grace with a ready smile. "I'm saving that for…"

"Ah yes," he cut in. "How could I forget? The riding club show. How is your schooling going, anyway?"

"Well, that's what I wanted to talk to you about," she said, seeing her opportunity. "I need some jumps, Dad."

"Mmmm," he made a face. "Sounds expensive."

"Not necessarily," she pleaded. "You could make some."

He took hold of his chin with thumb and forefinger, rolling his eyes. "Well, I don't know," he began.

"I'll get you a book with pictures to copy," she suggested. "Please, Dad…"

"How could I refuse my favorite girl anything," he laughed, ruffling her hair. "Come on, give me your saddle. You run on ahead and find that book before your mother gets back. I can't see her thinking that jumping will be a good idea."

"It's just because she doesn't understand horses," explained Grace in her mother's defense.

"And I do?" smiled her dad.

"Well…" She grimaced, splaying her palms. "You're getting better."

The jumps may have looked a bit strange, but they did the job. Within the next few days Todd Melrose had cut wood to make a couple of fillers and three sets of wings and bought a few poles from the local lumberyard. It had been Grace's job to paint them with any odd buckets of paint she could find around the house, and the result was the most garish and frightening-looking obstacles anyone could imagine.

She set them all out in the paddock that weekend, arranging and re-arranging them, before putting them all down to almost floor level and placing three trotting poles in a carefully measured outline.

"There," she announced out loud, pleased with the result.

When she went back into the house to get changed, her mother was in the kitchen, one elbow perched on the kitchen table and her chin resting on her upturned hand as she flicked over the page of what looked like a manual.

"Hello, hon," she said in a distracted tone.

Grace smiled. "I don't know," she remarked. "It's like living with a different person since you got that job."

Sue Melrose closed the book with a sigh. "Oh, I'm sorry, honey. I'm neglecting you, aren't I? It's just that there's so much to get through."

"Look, Mom," declared Grace, sitting down beside her for a moment. "I think it's really good that you have a job you enjoy, and I'm almost sixteen years old, remember. I can fend for myself a bit, you know."

Sue's pretty heart shaped face crinkled into a smile. "I know, hon, and I do appreciate it…"

"Well, then, open that book again and do your homework." Grace laughed.

"And I'll make you something nice for dinner," promised Sue. "Oh… and by the way," She hesitated, a slight flush coloring her pale skin, "your dad might be joining us."

Grace hugged her arms around herself as she ran up the stairs to change into her jodhpurs. She had put her scare on the shore behind her, her mother was happier at last and her dad even seemed to be getting fed up with the delectable Tina. Things seemed to be working out at last.

Their first jump schooling session could not have gone better, Grace thought as she turned on the shower a few hours later, reveling in the feel of hot water splashing over her skin.

She had spent over an hour just walking Magic around the paddock to let her see the crudely painted fences. At first, as she expected, the filly snorted, eyes on stalks, refusing to go anywhere near the brightly painted jumps, but she gradually relaxed, and by the end of the afternoon she was trotting willingly down the poles and even popping over some tiny fences. All in all, it had been a very satisfactory day, she decided, lathering her hair. And invisible sea horses felt a million miles away.

By the time she ran downstairs, still rubbing her shoulder length dark hair with a clean white towel, her mother had the table set and enticing aromas were floating out from the kitchen. The phone rang as she crossed the hall.

"Hi, Grace here."

"Sorry, love," replied her father's deep voice. "Something's come up. Tell your mom for me…"

As she put down the phone, Grace heard Tina's voice in the background. Her heart plummeted to her boots.

"Who was that, hon?" called her mother.

"Wrong number," she quickly responded, biting her lip. "I'm just going to check on Magic."

She ran around the side of the cottage, her cell phone already ringing. "You have to come Dad, it's not fair." Tears choked her throat. "Mom made dinner and everything."

"But…" he began.

"There are no buts," insisted Grace. "A promise is a promise."

There was a moment's heavy silence and then her father let out a deep sigh. "OK, fair enough. I didn't realize that it mattered so much."

"Well, it does."

"Tell her I'll be a bit late, then."

The phone went dead and when Grace burst back into

the house through the kitchen door her mother looked up from the stove, her smiling face pink with the heat. She ran the back of one hand across her forehead.

"Someone is in a hurry! Set the table for me, will you, hon?"

"Dad just called me on my cell phone," blurted out Grace. "He's going to be a little late."

Sue rolled her eyes. "Well, there's a surprise." she exclaimed. "I don't know why I bothered to ask him in the first place."

As she snuggled down beneath her comforter that night, watching the moon make patterns on the ceiling, Grace's mind flickered from Magic's first schooling session to their disastrous dinner that evening. Her father had been distracted and uneasy the whole time he was there, gulping his food and dashing off as soon as he had eaten.

"Well, that's the last time I try to build bridges," her mother had retorted as his car engine revved off down the lane.

Grace closed her eyes, focusing on her successful schooling session to fight off the disappointment. Vivid memories of looming cliffs and the cold, dark fathomless sea flooded her mind and she sat up suddenly. That was all behind her now, and she refused to think about it. She jumped out of bed and ran to the window, peering out into the moonlit night. Way, way off in the distance she could see lights bobbing on the sea, fishing boats catching the tide. Did they ever see mighty horses plunging through the waves, she wondered?

A cloud slipped over the silver moon, bringing a

heavy velvety darkness, and she climbed uneasily back into bed again. It was all nonsense, she told herself, and she had to try to control her vivid imagination before it drove her crazy.

She had seen the boy again today, the boy with the dog. Was he just in her imagination too, she wondered; had she gone completely crazy? He had raised a hand in greeting from across the short distance between them but she had simply gawked at him. Was he real, she wondered, and if he was, then where had he come from? Her eyes drooped shut as sleep came to claim her, bringing respite from her thoughts.

Little did she know that not so very far away, screened from the house by the high stone wall that surrounded the stable yard, Magic was also staring restlessly out into the night. Her pale head glistened in the light of the moon; nostrils flared and pointed ears sharply pricked toward the sea, listening for that distant sound again… The sound that had spooked her that day on the shore and was spooking her still… the sound that echoed above the waves, relentlessly drawing her in.

CHAPTER FIVE

Grace woke and stretched; one more day of school and it would be spring break. She brushed her teeth and dressed quickly, her mind still on yesterday's schooling session. Hope soared; maybe she and Magic would make her father proud after all.

"Your breakfast is on the table, and don't forget to lock the back door when you leave," called her mother. Her face appeared around the bedroom door and she lifted her fingers to her lips, blowing a kiss across the room. "And hurry up or you'll miss the bus."

"Bye, Mom," responded Grace with a smile. "See you tonight."

The school bus was already pulling up as she ran along the lane. She clambered aboard, feeling stupid, and collapsed onto the only available seat.

"You smell like horses," complained little Jimmy Mickleroy loudly. When everyone laughed she pushed her hands into her pockets, realizing that she had forgotten to wash them in the rush to catch the bus. Her face turned crimson as she stared determinedly out of the window. No wonder she didn't have any real friends; they all thought that she was weird… except for Nell, of course. She would tell her about it later if she saw her on the way to class. Anyway, she didn't care what they thought of her; there was Magic grazing in the paddock, a silvery white shape against the emerald green of the spring grass. She was worth a dozen friends.

"Well… horses smell nice, don't they?" consoled Nell as they hurried along the corridor forty-five minutes later. "Not that I've ever had much to do with them, of course."

Grace had come across her in the hall and blurted out her woes, desperate to share her embarrassing journey to school with someone.

"Maybe you could come to my house and see Magic some day," she suggested brightly, wondering if she dared to burden her new friend with the rest of her hidden worries. After all, she and Nell had kind of known each other for a few weeks now, but it had never gone further than kind of. Did she really want it to, though, wondered Grace as she made her impulsive offer. To her surprise, Nell went quiet and shook her head determinedly, her long blonde curly hair falling forward, hiding her expression.

"No… I can't… sorry. I'm a little scared of horses to be honest, and anyway, I have to get straight home after school."

"What…" Grace's dark eyebrows met in a puzzled frown. "Every day?"

Nell brushed her wayward hair back with her hand and shrugged. "I'm afraid so. It's my mom, you see... I'm her caretaker."

"Her caretaker! ... What? You mean that *you* have to look after your mom?"

"I don't mind," she quickly insisted. "There's no one else and she's in a wheelchair. She goes to the day center while I'm at school..."

They were mixed up then in a jumble of giggling teenagers hurrying to class, carried along with them to their desks on opposite sides of the room. Nell didn't *look* any different from the rest of the kids, thought Grace, glancing curiously across at her friend.

Mr. Mather's voice droned on and on in her ears about some long ago revolution as she peered around the class. All these teenagers hurried home after school to go out or to do their homework or to just hang out, she realized, but poor Nell had to stay in and look after her invalid mother. Maybe that's what had drawn them together in the first place; the fact that they were both different. Nell had to be responsible for her mother, and she was responsible for Magic; they both had something more important in their lives than the stuff the other kids did.

She went back to her work, trying to concentrate, but her mind just kept on whirling. Nell was small for her age, and slim. How could she actually care for an adult? And where was her dad, anyway? Grace had known her for over a month but she didn't actually *know* anything about her, she realized. Nell caught her gaze and smiled, the brightness in her blue eyes making her round plain face look almost pretty. She would spend some time with

48

her at lunchtime, decided Grace, and take a bit more interest; after all, what *did* they usually talk about? Guilt hit her. Did she just talk about Magic all the time?

As it was she didn't actually manage to speak to Nell again until the afternoon break, as she disappeared somewhere at lunchtime. When she did eventually find her friend she felt suddenly awkward and unsure of how to start.

So what is wrong with your mom, and will you have to care for her forever?

No… that was no good.

"I'm sorry about… you know," she eventually managed.

Nell smiled. "Sorry about what?"

Grace shrugged. "Sorry about not being more…"

"Look," Nell sat down on the wooden bench near the entrance to the gym, motioning Grace to sit beside her. "It's not your fault, and anyway I don't mind… well, not really."

"But you've never said anything, and I moan about my parents splitting up and brag about Magic all the time…"

"I like hearing about your horse," insisted Nell. "At least you have more in your life than making fun of someone or listening to the latest chart hits like most of the others around here, and I may have to look after my mom, but we're happy. My life is all mapped out, I decided ages ago. When I leave school I'm going to work with handicapped people, you know, train properly and everything. Anyway, I think I'm allergic to horses, so I couldn't come and see Magic, you see, even if I wanted to."

Grace thought about their conversation as she jumped

off the bus later that afternoon. Nell was her friend, she knew that, but they didn't really have much in common, apart from being different. Maybe she would understand though, about the crazy fears that haunted her dreams. If anything else happened then she would tell her at once, she decided, shivering suddenly as a wind whipped over the cliff top... The shiver tingled right down to her toes... That is, if she was *able* to tell her, she thought with a shudder.

The first day of vacation dawned, sunny and bright. *Just three more weeks until the show,* thought Grace as she hurried outside and ran along the path toward the low gray stone stable. Magic peered out over the half door. She whinnied when she saw her owner, and tossed her silvery head up and down.

"Breakfast's coming," called Grace, opening the door of the small shed that served as a feed room.

The filly ate nervously, grabbing a mouthful and turning her head to look outside, spilling feed all over the floor.

"What's wrong with you this morning, girl?" remarked Grace, patting her affectionately on the rump. As she set to work with her fork, lifting the droppings from the deep shavings bed, Magic fussed, shaking her whole body and moving from foot to foot.

"You must have been restless in the night," she exclaimed, looking at the disrupted bed with concern. Magic was usually so neat in the stable, but now the banks were down and white kick marks on the concrete wall told their own story. "No wonder you're agitated. Come on, let's have a look at you."

She ran her hand down each delicate looking limb,

feeling for lumps, bangs or heat. To her relief they all seemed totally cool and clean.

"No excuses then, girl," smiled Grace. "It's a schooling session for you this morning and then, just maybe, we really should think about going down to the shore again. It's time we laid a few ghosts to rest, don't you think?"

At first Magic seemed unwilling to concentrate, but Grace persisted, trotting over the poles again and again and bending her this way and that. Suddenly she moved away from the leg, stepping sideways without resistance and flexing her poll, accepting the rein.

"That's better, girl," murmured Grace with a smile as she floated forwards into a powerful rhythmic trot that made everything seem easy. "Maybe we should be doing dressage instead of jumping… or both, of course. What's your cross country like, I wonder?"

By lunchtime they were popping over the brightly colored fences in an easy, relaxed canter and Grace's heart began to sing. If Magic took to show jumping so easily then maybe they *could* do some horse trials one day.

Her confidence soared. "We'll show them, won't we, girl," she exclaimed, reining in and patting Magic's warm, damp neck. The aroma of horse assailed her nostrils and she took a deep breath; suddenly, for the very first time, she was actually looking forward to the riding club show.

After fifteen minutes of cooling down on a loose rein, Magic was so relaxed that the vague idea that had been whirling around in Grace's head had formulated into something positive. It was the right time; she knew it, the right time to face her stupid fears and ride down to the shore again. The right time to prove to herself that her terrifying experience a few short weeks ago would probably never happen again... the right time to put it behind her and move on.

Leaving Magic in her stable for a while, Grace raced into the house for a bag of chips and her cell phone. Darn, she'd attached it to the charger that morning but forgotten to switch the plug on. No matter, it was sure to have *some* life left in it. Of course she could leave it switched off, so that it was there just for an emergency. *No, that was stupid,* she told herself, slipping the phone into her pocket, like admitting that something might happen when she knew full well that it wouldn't.

Half an hour later, as Magic's hooves clip clopped down the narrow lane that led to the shore, Grace was smiling inside, knowing that she had made the right decision. The filly was so at ease that she couldn't imagine her getting the slightest bit spooked.

Ahead of them the sea glittered in the bright spring sunshine, gulls coasted overhead in easy circles, their high-pitched cries echoing in the clear air. Grace took a huge breath, suddenly so excited to be where she was at that moment in time.

"Come on, girl," she cried out, urging Magic into a trot. The filly responded half-heartedly, already tired from her session in the jumping paddock that morning, and Grace allowed her to walk again, feeling suddenly guilty. Maybe she was overdoing it; after all, Magic was only a four-year-old.

"I'll give you a day off tomorrow," she promised,

running one hand down her arched crest, "but we have to do this today, no matter what."

They passed the cottages, close to the paddock where the old lady saved Magic that day. What was her name? Grace reined in for a moment, trying to remember. Mollie, that was it, Mollie Jenkins. Two elderly men out for a stroll in the sunshine passed them.

"Lovely day," called the taller of the two, raising his cap to reveal a shiny, bald head.

Grace stifled a giggle and smiled broadly. "It's fantastic," she agreed. "By the way, you don't know which house Mollie Jenkins lives in, do you?"

The man turned to his white haired companion, eyebrows raised, then looked back at Grace with a shake of his head. "No... sorry. We have lived here for most of our lives but we've never heard of a Mollie Jenkins. Have a good ride, anyway."

"Thank you," responded Grace distractedly. She was sure that the old lady had told her she lived here... or had she? Never mind, although it would have been nice to say thank you.

She picked up her reins again, turning Magic's nose toward the shore. "Come on, girl. Do you think that you can summon up enough energy to canter?" The filly responded to her question by tossing her head eagerly and together they began the steep descent to the narrow strip of sand that stretched along beneath the looming cliffs like a golden pathway.

The tide was high. *Coming in or going out?* Grace wondered. She should have remembered that although the tides weren't quite as high as they had been three

53

weeks ago, they still came very close to the base of the cliffs. She could see the sea from her bedroom window, but had the tide been in or out when she woke up that morning? Her mind had been too distracted by her plans for the day to notice, she realized. Never mind. They would have to be quick, that's all, just to be sure.

Magic's hooves left the rough stone of the trail for the smooth, damp sand, eerily soundless on its crumbling surface. She lifted her head, silvery mane blowing in the breeze and dark eyes raised almost longingly toward the distant horizon. Sensing her tension Grace leaned forwards, placing an understanding hand on the silky smoothness of her neck, absorbing her warmth and breathing in her familiar horsy aroma.

"What's up, girl? Don't worry, everything will be fine this time... you'll see."

A gull swooped down, its screaming cry echoing mournfully into the wind, huge wings flapping easily as it coasted along beside them.

"Come on," Grace said, elation flooding her veins as she breathed in the magic of the moment. They were all alone on the golden stretch of sand. The sea sang a gentle, soothing song and beside them the awesome cliffs rose into a clear blue sky. Her calves wrapped themselves around Magic's sides, her fingers closed on the reins and she leaned forward into the breeze as the horse beneath her leaped into motion. Suddenly all her fears disappeared. Nothing mattered but the feel of the wind in her face and the sheer power that carried her along the shoreline. She was one with the wind, with the sea, with the world, another being in a different place where adrenalin flooded her senses.

The roar that filled her head came so suddenly that it happened as if in a dream. *Was it the sea that called, or the sky beyond?* The roar became a cry that she had heard before, in dreams. It was vaguely, almost comfortingly, familiar; a screaming neigh that filled every orifice of her being.

Magic heard it too. Grace felt the bulge of muscles beneath her as the filly's whole body froze in mid-gallop.

It happened in slow motion, with no time to think or act. One moment they were pounding along the beach, totally overtaken by the sheer exhilaration of speed, and in the next... in the next the silver filly was spinning, throwing her body sideways, slithering to a halt... just like the last time.

Grace hung on, determination overcoming the force that threw her from side to side. She wrapped her fingers into Magic's mane and clung, her legs vice-like around her horse's heaving sides. And then the whole world was spinning as confusion robbed her of her bearings. The cry came again, a deep rumbling cry that was at one with the waves, a part of the sea, and yet... It filled the air around them, becoming a part of them, a sound that held the crash of the waves and the roar of the mighty sea; a sound that rose to a crescendo, all its power ringing out at last into the longest, loneliest, screaming whinny she had ever heard.

In the moment before the cry faded, leaving an empty silence, Grace felt such a sad sense of loneliness flood over *her* that fear faded. Beneath her Magic trembled, deflated like a pricked balloon, as if all her energy had been sapped away by the mighty force of emotion in the sound that had filled their senses.

Amazingly, the sky was still calm and blue with one fluffy white cloud floating gently across the sun. The sea sparkled with tranquility; the pale cliffs loomed, firm and solid, and the golden sand stretched smoothly out before them. Was this a dream, she wondered? Would she wake in a moment, warm in her bed, shuddering with relief?

When Magic sidled beneath her, snorting nervously, she closed her fingers so tightly on the leather reins that her fingernails marked the balls of her thumbs. No, she realized as fear flooded back, this was no dream. All around them were hoof prints, just like before. Hoof prints surrounded them… Hoof prints that came out of the sea and… for a fleeting moment she closed her eyes, not daring to look… Hoof prints that had no beginning … and no end… and went back into the waves again.

Grace rode home on automatic, trying to focus her thoughts on anything but her crazy experience; could there really be a mighty horse out there, and who would believe her if she told them? She stifled the thought, mentally squashing it. She had survived, that was what mattered, and she hadn't fallen off this time, either. The show, that was it, she needed to concentrate on her preparation for the show. Maybe her dad could make some more jumps… Her mind whirled, confused by images of colorful fences superimposed upon visions she dared not face.

There were the two old men again, still walking slowly along the headland, passing by as if nothing had happened… But nothing had happened… had it?

Grace smiled at them vacantly, just as if she was a normal person out for a ride on a clear, sunny afternoon.

"Did you find your Mollie Jenkins?" asked the taller of the two, doffing his cap as before. He had kind eyes and a gentle smile… Could she tell *him*?

"Uh… no," she eventually spluttered, rejecting the idea.

At least she could still speak … and breathe… and feel… and see. She was alive, that was what mattered… but had she ever imagined that she wouldn't be? The mighty horse had saved her life once, so why would it hurt her now? There, she had admitted to herself that there really was a mighty horse. Somewhere in the deep swell of the ocean there was… She shivered and blinked hard, taking a breath.

"Good luck, my dear," called the second man and she smiled again, drifting back into the present; at least they were on their way home, safe and sound.

Beneath her Magic also shivered and she patted her shoulder. "Don't worry, girl, we'll be home soon. Everything is going to be fine, you'll see."

But was it? Would anything ever be fine again? She urged the tired filly into a trot, eager to get back, to tell someone, to share her awesome experience with… with whom? Whom *could* she talk to? Who would listen?

The dark haired boy watched her pass by, longing to approach her but unsure of his reception. He threw a stick for the big gray dog that clung to him like a shadow. Maybe he should just go and tell her now. After all, wasn't it her right to know? Magic trotted briskly on and he hesitated. He would tell her when the time was right.

CHAPTER SIX

Magic steamed gently, clouds of vapor rising into the clear air as Grace brushed her coat the wrong way and threw on a cooler, taking comfort in normal, everyday actions. The empty driveway had brought a rush of disappointment. She had imagined running in to see her mother, blurting out her terror, sharing her fears, but no; the empty gray tarmac stared at her, dotted with the weeds she had promised to pull up two days ago. There was no one home to tell.

Maybe it was good thing, she decided as she made up Magic's feed. Maybe she should try to get her own head straight before she tried to explain it to anyone else.

She bolted the door firmly, double-checking on the kick bolt. *The mighty sea spirit may not want to harm her, but what about Magic?* There, she had admitted it to herself, admitted that she believed in the mystical horse that rode the waves and left hoof prints in the sand; admitted that it really had saved her life that day.

She would tell her father, she decided, heading for the cottage, or her mother; whichever parent she saw first, in fact.

Something on the table caught her attention as she entered the kitchen; a note, held down by a porcelain pig and fluttering in the draught from the open door. The door banged shut behind her and the note went still, a white patch against the warm yellow pine. Grace read it quickly.

"I'll be back around 6:30 with fish and chips for dinner. Love Mom. XX"

She glanced at her watch; one and a half hours to go, one and a half hours before she could talk to her mother. Clicking down the names in her cell phone, she paused with her finger above Dad before snapping it shut and reaching up into the cupboard for a bag of chips. Her dad would still be at work; she would just have to wait.

Half an hour later Grace sat in front of the flickering TV screen with no idea of what program was on. Her mind was a million miles away, going through every moment of her experience on the shore again and again, and every time the same thought kept coming back again: the mighty sea horse, or whatever it was, really had saved her that day in the sea. It had buoyed her up above the waves and taken her safely to the shore. And yet there was something else, some looming awesome power that hovered, just out of reach, waiting for… waiting for what?

From outside the open window she heard Magic's cry, a high-pitched restless whinny, calling for…?

The answer hit like a punch in the stomach, leaving a churning apprehension that turned her blood cold. Of course, why hadn't she already seen it? The spirit from the sea didn't want *her*... it wanted... It wanted her lovely silver filly, and that was why she was so afraid of it. She was afraid for Magic, not herself.

Magic whinnied again, a lonely cry that echoed into the silence of the night, rattling around inside Grace's head. Way, way off in the distance, she thought she heard a rumbling response... Or was it just the crashing of the waves against the tall limestone cliffs? Suddenly, for the first time ever, Beachy Heights seemed a very lonely place to be.

By the time Sue came home, Magic's top door was securely bolted, and Grace was beginning to think that maybe she had overreacted just a bit. All that business with Tina, followed by her scare on the shore must be driving her crazy, she decided.

"Hello, hon, had a good day?" asked her mother, depositing an armful of groceries on the table. When Grace automatically began putting it away, she took hold of her daughter's arm. "Leave that for now. I've got fish and chips here; they'll be cold if we don't eat them now. I'll put the kettle on while you get some plates out."

Grace's stomach churned at the delicious aroma and she hurried to do her mother's bidding. When did she get so hungry?

It wasn't until after they had eaten that Grace finally managed to get her mother's attention. She poured out her heart, leaving nothing back, and when she eventually fell silent, Sue sat very still for a moment, digesting her daughter's wild story.

"So!" she eventually exclaimed, her face impassive and her brow slightly furrowed, as if looking for the right response. She had sat and listened patiently to her daughter's dramatic account of her adventures, and now she needed to think it through.

"…So," she repeated. "You really think that there's something out there … some kind of mighty horse spirit of the sea, you mean?"

Grace shrugged. It had all seemed to make sense until she told her mother, and now it seemed a bit, well, weird.

"Look," Sue sipped her coffee. "Think about it practically… You went out that first time and Magic misbehaved. That's not so strange, is it? She is four years old, and all that wide-open space – not to mention the crashing waves – probably just panicked her. Anyway, when you fell you must have hit your head to make you decide to do that crazy climb in the first place; all I can say is thank heaven the tide came in…"

"But what about…?" cut in Grace.

Her mother raised a hand, silencing her.

"I was coming to that, and just listen, I think it makes sense. I do believe that you were washed up onto the shore, but because you were only half-conscious, maybe you only *imagined* the great horse spirit that saved you." Reaching out a hand, she ran the back of her fingers across Grace's pink cheek. "You really will have to stop all this crazy nonsense, you know, hon."

"But what about today?" blurted out Grace, unconvinced. "And what about the hoof prints that lead to nowhere?"

"Look," Sue's chair scraped on the tiles as she stood

up. "I don't know much about horses, but surely if a nervous young filly like Magic has had a scare, she's not going to forget about it easily. She remembered, that's all, remembered what happened the first time you went down on the shore. And as for the hoof prints... Well, to be honest, hon, don't you think that there are other people riding along there, who maybe canter their horses through the waves... you know... in and out again?"

Suddenly Grace felt so foolish. Her mother's practical reasoning made all her wild fears seem totally stupid. "I guess you could be right," she agreed with a relieved smile.

"Well then, let's get our supper and forget all about it. There's some show jumping on the TV later."

"And you're not going to make me sell Magic?

Her mother hesitated.

"I'm worried, of course," she admitted. "But I know how much you love her. What I *am* going to do, though, is ask you not to ride down onto the shore again... You've had a warning, so please take note of it."

"Just try and make me," laughed Grace. "I don't think I'll even be walking down there for a while."

As Grace's body brush swept across Magic's silvery coat in sweeping strokes – one... two... three... and across the currycomb – all her thoughts channeled toward the riding club show. Two weeks, that's all it was, and every time she thought about it her heart began to pound. She had never been in any kind of horse competition before, not even mounted games, so to actually be going to jump was just so exciting.

The *what ifs* spiraled in from a sheltered corner of her mind but she pushed them determinedly aside, remembering an article she once read in a horse magazine. It was all about positive thinking. You had to *imagine* yourself doing something well again and again; clearing obstacles, overcoming problems, and on the morning of the show you were to go over every fence in your mind, jumping it with ease.

"There," she finally announced, putting down her grooming kit and standing back to survey the results of her handiwork.

"She looks like a picture," announced her father's voice from just behind her.

Grace looked around with a smile. She hadn't seen him all weekend, and she longed to know what had happened with Tina.

"I'll just put her rug back on and then you can tell me all about it," she announced.

"All about what?" Her father's face was deliberately blank.

"Oh no," she wailed. "Please don't tell me that you're back together?"

Todd shook his head firmly. "No… don't worry, love, that's all behind me now. No fool like an old fool, eh?"

"You can say that again," remarked Grace, shaking her head. "Come on, Mom will be back from the shop soon. Time for you to start building bridges."

"It will have to be a very large bridge," he groaned. "Oh, and by the way, she called and told me about your fall and trying to climb up the cliff. You could have been killed, you idiot. Why didn't you tell *me* about it?"

Grace slipped the bolt on the stable door and flipped over the kick bolt before falling into step beside him. "I tried to," she admitted, suddenly feeling so relieved that her awesome secret was out *and* so easily explained away. Why had she kept it to herself for so long?

"Well, next time…" he began, just as his cell phone rang out in a lively, modern tune.

He pulled it from his pocket, grimaced at her and held it to his ear. Grace sighed as she saw his expression change.

"I'll be there in a minute… Don't do anything stupid."

As he turned back toward her the guilty look in his eyes told all.

"Tina?" she groaned.

His lips brushed her forehead. "Sorry, love. I'll be back later… promise!"

Despite her mother's reassuring explanation, when Grace suddenly woke in the early hours of the morning to see shadows moving across her bedroom ceiling, the heart-stopping panic came rushing back. The moon was high in the sky, and its eerie glow cast a pale silver light against which loomed the great black shapes of the trees beyond her window. They moved ominously in the breeze, like living things against the sky, and she shuddered, pulling her comforter up close around her chin.

Was that a cry?

She jumped out of bed and ran to the window, peering out into the weird, magical night. No, all seemed quiet and calm. Her mother was right, she decided, she was just way too over imaginative. Back in bed again she snuggled down and turned her thoughts to the terrifying events of her first ride down to the shore, remembering her fall and her crazy climb and that half-forgotten journey through the rolling sea.

In the hazy moments before sleep, she felt the powerful surge beneath her again... long tendrils of mane against her face... a great arched neck... No! Sleep drained away. She had been only half-conscious, remember, which is why her memories were just vague physical impressions without shape or form. She was lucky to be alive, truly, but it was good luck that had saved her from drowning and nothing else.

Turning her thoughts to the show next month, she put everything else out of her head as her eyelids began to droop again. Yesterday was forgotten as a big mistake; tomorrow was what really counted, and the days that followed... Yet still yesterday lurked, despite her resolve, a secret unfinished mystery that was a part of the future she was trying to avoid.

Sleep closed over her, sweet and calming, a respite from the world. Tomorrow was another day, with new goals and new frontiers...

Little did Grace know that in the small stable yard beyond the wall, behind the securely fastened door, Magic stood stock-still, dark eyes shining and pointed ears pricked sharply toward the sea. Way, way off in the distance she listened for the deep, rumbling cry again, the cry that called out to her, drawing her in.

The empty crashing of the waves against the awesome limestone cliffs mingled with the sound so that both became one, the mighty roar of the sea and the great deep whinny, indistinguishable from one another. Moving restlessly around her stable the silver filly pawed at the bed of shavings beneath her hooves, piling it into mounds as her heart raced with excitement... For the sound was calling her home, to the only place she wanted to be.

CHAPTER SEVEN

"What have you been up to?" exclaimed Grace, staring in horror at Magic's disturbed bed. She had woken up refreshed after her mother's sound advice last night, but now alarm bells rang again.

She slipped on a head collar and then unfastened Magic's rug, pulling it off to reveal streaks of dried sweat on the filly's pale coat.

"You must have been restless again," she announced with dismay. "Are you colicky?"

Magic tossed her head, calmer now that morning had dawned; the events of the night were a distant dream, and breakfast was here.

She snorted softly, plunging her nose into the fragrant smelling bucket while Grace carefully looked her over.

"Well, you seem fine now," she announced with relief, patting her neck. "Do you feel up to doing some schooling after breakfast?"

Magic ignored her, intent upon eating, and Grace set to work with her fork.

"Maybe I should get you a dietary supplement," she remarked while deftly separating the soiled parts from the messed up bed. "Pro-biotics or something. I'll take a look in my horse magazines."

Less than an hour later Grace's worries about her horse's health were put on hold as she trotted Magic around the paddock beside the cottage. Magic was doing so well that there couldn't possibly be anything wrong with her, Grace decided. A breeze stirred the tree tops and a dark cloud just above them threatened rain but she was totally oblivious to anything but the feel of the horse beneath her, especially when Magic popped willingly down a line of bounce fences for the very first time. Grace turned her horse toward them again, reveling in the ease with which she sprang over the cross poles.

"You are a star," she exclaimed, pulling up near the gate. "Come on, let's try something a bit bigger."

She slipped to the ground, looped the reins over her arms, led Magic across to a spread fence that was set apart from the grid and raised the red and white back pole a hole.

"What do you think, girl?" she asked.

Magic just grabbed for grass, ignoring her, and on a sudden impulse she lifted the pole two more.

"Come on, then!" she cried out and, placing her toe in the stirrup, she sprang lightly into the saddle, gathering up her reins with a fierce determination. "Let's see what you're really made of."

Sensing her rider's apprehension Magic tossed her

head and blew through her nostrils, champing on the bit as she eased toward the gate. Flecks of white foam splattered from her mouth, billowing away on the breeze like snow.

"Come on," pleaded Grace, urging her determinedly forward. "Don't let me down now."

For just a moment more the filly hesitated, but then she suddenly relaxed, moving smoothly forward and flicking neatly into a rhythmic canter. Grace sat up, trying to stay calm as they approached the red and white triple bar she had just altered. Suddenly it looked huge.

"Legs on," she breathed, feeling the stride through her seat.

One… two… three… The power of the take-off took her by surprise, and she threw herself forwards and grabbed a chunk of mane, almost losing her balance in the explosion of Magic's jump. Her heart was racing as they landed neatly and moved away. There was no doubt about it; her beautiful Thoroughbred filly really could perform.

"We'll show them, won't we, girl?" she cried out, laughing out loud with delight as adrenalin flooded her veins. The riding club show was becoming more appealing every minute, mysterious sea horses seemed a million miles away, and tomorrow beckoned enticingly.

"Just a few more fences and you can cool off with a walk along the lane," she promised, heading for the red and white fence again.

"Had a successful day, darling?" asked her mother later that evening.

Grace looked up from her homework with a smile. "Terrific, actually," she announced, putting down her pen.

Sue nodded. "Good, no more silly worries about magic sea horses, then?"

Grace stood up and began putting her books back into her school bag. "I think that episode is well behind me," she laughed. "What's for dinner?"

It was nice to just feel normal again, she decided, settling down in front of the TV, and tomorrow, at school, she would to tell Nell all about her crazy experiences, and they could have a real laugh about it.

To her surprise her small, serious faced friend just frowned when her story came to an end. She had told her everything – all about falling and climbing the cliff and imagining that she had been saved by some kind of great sea horse, but, to her dismay, Nell didn't even smile.

"So, she repeated. "My Mom says that I must just have had a concussion. I'll never be so lucky again, I can tell you."

"Maybe it wasn't just luck?"

At her friend's remark, Grace's heart flipped over. "What do you mean, it wasn't just luck? Are you trying to say that you think there's some truth to it?"

Nell's eyes were wide, her mouth a taut line. "Well… no, except, well there is that old legend."

Grace gawped at her. "Legend…?"

"I don't know the details. It's… well…" She hesitated, doubt clouding her pale face.

"Go on," insisted Grace.

"It's an old story… about a great horse that haunts the coast around here."

"You *are* joking," exclaimed Grace as something squeezed her guts… *Please, please let her be joking*.

"I'll ask my mom," promised Nell, trying to smile away her worried frown. "She reads a lot and she knows all sorts of things about the history around here."

"You *were* just playing with me, weren't you?" asked Grace again as they hurried along the corridor to their next class.

Nell shrugged. "It was just something that came into my head, something I once heard. I shouldn't have said anything. I'll ask my Mom tonight, though. Don't worry, I've probably remembered it totally wrong."

Despite her friend's advice not to worry, the expression on her face just kept on coming back into Grace's mind. Her father came by after school and wanted to see her jumping Magic, so she duly tacked the filly up and took her over all the fences again, but her performance was lackluster compared to the day before.

"You seem a little out of sorts, love," remarked Todd.

He was leaning against the gate, chewing on a piece of grass, and Grace walked Magic toward him, wondering whether or not to tell him what Nell had said.

Resisting the temptation, she urged the filly into a canter, popped her down the grid again and headed for the triple bar, totally missing her stride. The back pole fell with a clang.

"Back to the drawing board," smiled her father. "Come on, your mother has kindly offered me some supper so we'd better not be late."

* * * * *

It seemed like an eternity before Grace got the chance to speak to Nell again, since her friend was late for school next morning. She came running into the science lab after the class had started. Miss Mills looked down her long nose with disgust, but then hesitated.

"Ah… Nell Gibson…" she remarked, waiting for her excuse.

Nell's face was crimson. "Sorry," she stuttered. "They were late coming to get my mom and I missed the first bus."

Miss Mills' stern face softened and she nodded her gray head. "How is your mother, dear?" she asked kindly.

"She's OK," mumbled Nell, hating the attention and scuttling to her seat.

Grace found it hard to concentrate and the more she stared at the print before her on the desk, the more her mind wandered, going through all the things she had been trying to put out of her head. She didn't want this, didn't want her stomach to keep churning. Suddenly she felt angry at Nell for putting doubts in her mind.

"So what do *you* think, Grace Melrose?"

At the sound of Miss Mills' sharp voice, her heart skipped a beat.

"Um…" she began vaguely, looking helplessly down at the blur of words before her.

"I think you will find that we are a couple of pages further on," barked her stern-faced teacher. "If you aren't going to concentrate here, then maybe you had better stay back in detention."

Grace's face turned a fiery red. "Sorry, Miss Mills," she stuttered.

The rest of the lesson dragged, and as soon as they were outside in the spring sunshine she turned to Nell.

"Well?" she asked. "What did your mom say?"

"It's a bit weird, really," she responded cautiously, flicking back her long blonde hair. "My mom says that there *is* an old story about a great sea horse. It's supposed to have been sighted way out in the ocean, and there are reports of a screaming whinny. But you shouldn't worry too much, because it's probably just an old wives' tale. There are loads of those around here; it's because of all the poor sad people who have jumped off the cliffs. If you think about it the white breakers could easily be mistaken for a mighty horse with a flowing mane and gulls often sound odd when a storm is due, especially when people are feeling emotional. That's not really what's weird."

Grace took hold of her sleeve. "What do you mean… what *is* weird, then?"

"It's your horse's name," continued Nell.

"What, you mean, Magic?"

"No… not just Magic. *Heathwaite* Magic."

"What about it?" asked Grace cautiously?

"Well…" Nell looked at her from under her lashes. "My mom says that there is a place near here with that name, a place that used to breed some of the best horses in the country until they had bad luck. The ancestors live there still, just a few miles along the coast. Heathwaite Hall, it's called, but she doesn't know the name of the people."

Grace looked at her with a puzzled expression in her clear gray eyes. "But what does that have to do with the horse from the sea?"

Nell hoisted her bag further back on her shoulder. "Well… nothing, probably. It's just that the tale of the sea horse in the bay has something to do with their bad luck. Maybe there's a link."

"So you are saying that there might be some truth in it?"

"No," responded Nell, too quickly. "I just think that it might be interesting to go to Heathwaite Hall and find out if there *is* a link between your Magic and the horses that were bred there, that's all."

"Can you come with me?"

Even as she asked Grace knew that it was impossible. Nell's face fell and she squeezed her shoulder. "Don't worry, I know you can't. I'll just ride over and have a look."

The idea preyed on Grace's mind all morning; at least it would be something positive to do. She would go on the weekend, she decided, and until then she would stay well away from the shore.

Magic seemed more settled over the next couple of days. Grace schooled her a few times in the paddock in the evenings, and on Thursday she decided to ride along the cliff top pathway.

She saw the boy again, throwing a stick for his dog across the smooth sweep of coarse grass above the cliff top. When he raised a hand in greeting, she waved back. *Who is he*, she wondered, *and where is he from?* There was something about him, something familiar and appealing. Maybe she should go and speak to him.

Magic spooked at an invisible monster. Grace kicked her forward into a trot and the moment was gone. Next time, then, she decided. The next time she saw the boy she would introduce herself.

The sky was a silvery gray with streaks of purple on the horizon, the kind of sky that you could only ever see above the sparkling expanse of the sea. Grace breathed in deeply, taking in the smell of salty air and the ever present distant aroma of fish – or was it just the smell of the sea?

Below her, tiny white breakers crashed against the shore, and she smiled to herself. What was she thinking? Mighty horses plunging through the waves! She must be going crazy! No wonder her mother had laughed it off. This business of Heathwaite Hall, however, now that was interesting. Maybe whoever lived there now would be able to tell her the tale of the sea horse and the cause of the bad luck that made them disband the stud farm. Nell said that it was just a few miles further along the path she was following, looking right down across the ocean. Suddenly she felt nervous at the prospect of going there alone, but she was determined to do it.

"First thing on Saturday morning, girl," she told Magic, who tossed her head and broke into a jog.

It wasn't until they turned toward home that Grace noticed the tension in her horse's body, a kind of nervousness. It was just as the path ran close to the edge of the cliff. The familiar fear prickled and she brushed it aside, nudging her forward to trot.

"Come on, girl," she cried. "Let's go home."

The sound took her by surprise, filling her head for just a moment. It rose above the crash of the waves below, deeper than the melancholy cries of the gulls that coasted overhead; a rumbling whinny that came from nowhere and struck a chord in her horse's heart. One minute they were trotting calmly along the pathway and the next Magic was heading for the cliff top. Grace hauled on the reins, screaming at her, and suddenly she stopped. The sea below was calm, the swish of the breeze caressed Grace's face, and beneath her Magic's sides heaved.

"What is going on with you, girl?" sighed Grace. Maybe it was she who was going crazy. She pricked her ears, listening for the sound again, but even the wind was suddenly quiet.

"It has to be my imagination," she announced, heading for home. "Maybe that knock on the head did more damage than I thought. Or maybe someone around here has a horse."

The smooth green of the cliff top, dotted with stunted trees, stretched before her and discounted that idea. She sighed, pushing aside her secret fear… the terrifying fear that it was all true, that maybe both she and her horse were in danger. But then again, she couldn't be, could she? She had faced death that day in the water and something had saved her. She must never forget that.

Grace noticed her father's black sports car in the driveway as Magic's hooves clip clopped around the final corner to where their low-roofed white cottage greeted her. A warm feeling calmed her jangling nerves, a kind of safe familiarity. Maybe he and her mom really would make up one day and then they could all be together, here in the place she had grown to love. At least something good had come out of the heartache of the last months; if her parents hadn't split up she would not have come to Sea View Cottage, not have even seen the cliffs at Beachy Heights.

Did something good always come out of something bad, she wondered? Maybe that was it. Maybe when something bad happened you should immediately start looking for the good.

"Nice ride, love?"

Her father leaned on the gate, a broad smile plastered across his handsome face.

"Yes," she smiled. "Where's Mom?"

"Making dinner. She asked me to come and look out for you."

Her face brightened. "Are you staying again?"

"Certainly am," he grinned. "But don't get your hopes up. It'll take a lot more time to make your mother forgive me."

Grace jumped down from the saddle and ran up her stirrups. "And what about Tina?" she asked quietly.

Her father shrugged. "Oh, that's all in the past," he insisted, unbuckling Magic's girth and sliding off her saddle. "I told you, just a silly mistake," then he hoisted it over his arm and headed off toward the house.

"And don't be too long; it's almost ready," he called back over his shoulder.

Grace watched him go with a sigh. Why did grown ups always make such a mess of everything?

CHAPTER EIGHT

The day was disappointingly gray and drizzle rimed Magic's coat, bringing a sparkle to the silver as Grace headed her along the lane. She shook her head and droplets fell from the edge of her riding hat.

Oh, why did it have to rain today? She sighed, peering through the mist. A car approached with its headlights glaring and she pulled into the gateway. Magic had been very good in traffic up to now, but there *was* a limit.

When the car swished by, engine humming, Magic snorted loudly and Grace patted her neck. Her hand made a satisfying slapping sound upon the filly's slippery wet coat. "Now don't you go letting me down again," she pleaded, heading her back out into the lane.

All week it had been blustery and bright, but when Grace woke that morning to the rumble of thunder and the patter of raindrops upon her window, she had found herself wondering if she should leave her outing until tomorrow. No! She had jumped out of bed before she could change her mind. Today she was going to find Heathwaite Hall as planned, no matter what, and a little rain wasn't going to stop her.

Her mother was working so there was no one to question her whereabouts, and she had fed and mucked out early. At least Magic seemed calm and relaxed today, she noted thankfully. The filly demurely stepped from her stable. It was bad enough riding out in the wind and rain as it was, and the last thing Grace needed was for her to be in one of her lively moods.

They set off along the lane in good spirits and by the time they reached the road that led all the way along the top of the cliffs, the rain had abated a little. Grace twisted in the saddle to look around her. The whole world seemed to be hidden in a misty cloud that had swallowed all the familiar landmarks. She shivered, concentrating on forwards again, and was suddenly hit by the crazy idea that she was in a whole different world.

"Come on, girl," she announced, wanting to break the silence. Magic dutifully broke into a brisk trot and she went with the filly's elevated pace, knees and ankles springing as she reveled in the powerful movement beneath her.

According to Nell's mom, Heathwaite Hall was about three miles along the cliff top road. Grace glanced at her watch; surely they must be almost there by now. As if on cue the mist slowly lifted, fading away to reveal the smooth green sweep of the grassland that sloped down toward the awesome, unfenced drop of the cliff face. Way, way below the sea sparkled and just a bit further along, set back in its own grounds, was an impressive stone house with a cluster of buildings nestling behind it. Could that be? she wondered, heart in mouth. Could she really be lucky enough to have found it so easily? Now what?

Magic tossed her head, eager to turn around and head home, but Grace closed her hands firmly on the reins. She hadn't thought further than actually getting here. What had she expected to find, anyway? Should she just knock on the impressive front door and ask if the occupant knew anything about an old legend attached to the property? She imagined herself doing just that and balked at the idea, glancing nervously around to see a small wooden sign that read, *Bridle path*. It pointed into the meadow beside the hall, appearing to lead right past the front door. Maybe if she followed it she might come across someone and... and what? She would cross that bridge when she came to it, she decided, already reaching down to open the wicket gate.

The route seemed to cross the meadow before turning back to follow what appeared to be the garden wall, and Grace set off eagerly, grateful for the sun that had suddenly burst from its confining cloud to bring a whole new feel to the morning. Magic swung along in a leisurely walk and her confidence soared. Maybe she *would* ask... if she saw anyone, that was.

They were halfway across the wide-open space when she felt Magic tense beneath her. Gulls coasted overhead and at first she thought that it was just their shrieking cries she could hear, spooking the high-strung filly... until she heard another sound, high pitched and distinctive.

Her whole body tightened and her breath seemed to be momentarily trapped in her lungs as she froze in the saddle. Magic wheeled around, ears pricked and muscles bulging. For a second that seemed to last a lifetime, Grace clung on helplessly; she had to do something before the horse beneath her erupted, plunging and leaping like the last time. Determination flooded her senses, overriding fear. She kicked Magic forward, keeping a firm hold on the slippery reins as she tried to circle, but Magic ignored her. Pricking her sharply pointed ears she leaped forward into full gallop, faster and faster, straight down the slope toward… Grace clawed at the reins in panic as the wind whipped against her face… toward the cliff. She was heading straight for the edge of the cliff.

The whole thing seemed to be happening in slow motion. All Grace could think of was her mother and her father, waiting hopelessly for her to come home, searching for her along the cliff top…

Frantically she tried to turn, leaning dangerously forward to grab the bit ring, desperation lending strength… to no avail. Maybe she should just throw herself off now, at full gallop. Surely a broken arm or leg would be better that plummeting down that awesome drop. The ground flashed by, the sound of hooves thudded in time with her heartbeat and even as she poised herself for the inevitable, suddenly she began hauling on the reins again, knowing that she had to try and save her precious horse.

Just when she thought it was too late, when the edge of the cliff loomed in front of Magic's flying hooves, something leaped toward them; a large dark shape

barking furiously – huge white fangs – a flash of red from a gaping mouth. Magic turned abruptly, shocked from her crazy flight, stopping as quickly as she had started to stand with sides heaving. Grace slid to the ground, legs buckling beneath her as she gasped for breath.

"Are you totally crazy? You could have been killed!"

The voice from behind her took her by surprise. Where was the dog? Had she dreamed it? Or had they already made the awesome leap and this was some kind of crazy afterworld?

Firm fingers took hold of Magic's rein, and she dropped her head toward the grass as if it was just a normal day. Had the whole world gone totally crazy?

A long warm tongue brought Grace back to reality, licking her face with delight. For a moment she closed her eyes; the world may be crazy but this was real. She was alive and her precious horse was safe.

"Get off her, Buster," chortled the friendly voice again and she took a breath, struggling to see the tall boy from the other day staring down at her with dark, friendly eyes. They twinkled, she noted. She had never seen eyes that actually twinkled before.

"Now maybe you can explain why you keep on riding all alone along the cliff top on a totally crazy Thoroughbred," he smiled. "Or were you trying to commit suicide?"

"I…" she began, looking at him with surprise. "But, how do you know that she's a Thoroughbred?"

The boy rolled his eyes. "I've seen enough pictures of top-class Thoroughbreds in my gran's house to recognize one when I see it. In fact…"

He stood back, looking Magic over.

"There is one picture that's almost identical. Heathwaite Magic Moment; the resemblance is uncanny."

The blood in Grace's veins seemed to turn suddenly icy cold.

"But *she's* called Heathwaite Magical Mist," she breathed, meeting his intense gaze.

"Then there must be a link," he remarked practically. "And that *is* weird, because the stud was disbanded years ago. The very first time I saw you, though, I thought the filly looked familiar, and then I realized why. I was going to tell you before, but you always seemed so, well…"

"Well, what?" retorted Grace.

Suddenly the huge gray dog burst in between them, breaking the tension. He dropped a stick at his master's feet and the boy picked it up and hurled it in the direction of the house.

"Come on," he insisted, changing the subject. "Let's go inside. My gran would be the best person to talk to. She knows all about the horses and the old legends."

"Old legends?" cut in Grace. "What legends?"

"I think you need to sit down and have a drink first," he smiled, "and my name is Jack, by the way."

"Grace," she told him. "I'm Grace Melrose, and…" She lowered her eyes, suddenly feeling awkward. "Thank you for saving me."

"More like Grace MAD rose, the way you rode down that hill," he laughed, "and it's not me you should be thanking, it's Buster here."

Grace fell to her knees, cradling the huge gray Irish

wolfhound's head in her hands. "Thank you, Buster," she said, suddenly smiling.

Jack's gran wasn't home when they went into the huge old-fashioned kitchen.

"She'll probably be back soon," he remarked. "I'll go put the kettle on. Hot chocolate all right?"

Grace nodded. She suddenly felt totally worn out. "Yes, thanks."

He motioned her toward a rocking chair next to the black range. "You'd better sit down, and don't worry about your precious Magic. She'll be fine in that old stable. It must be years since it had a horse in it, but it used to be a stallion box."

Suddenly Grace felt uneasy, as if her whole world was about to change… but then again she realized… it had already changed.

Five minutes later, with Buster's huge head resting on her knee and a warm mug of hot chocolate cradled in her hands, Grace felt a whole lot better.

"Now," remarked Jack firmly. "I think you had better tell me what the problem is."

"Problem!" responded Grace nervously.

"Yes, Grace MAD rose, the problem that brought you here and made your crazy horse almost jump over the cliff."

Grace glanced up into his twinkling dark eyes and immediately looked away. "You'll think that I'm crazy too if I tell you."

"Try me," he insisted.

She looked back at him at him, long and hard. Did she dare, really dare, to unburden herself to a stranger? Still, how could he be a stranger when he had saved her life? Anyway, she had seen him before. "It started on the first day that I decided to ride Magic down to the shore…" she began.

When the torrent of words Jack's kindness had unleashed finally dried up, a deep silence fell between the two young people who huddled next to the warmth of the ancient black range. It was Grace who broke it first. Her voice sounded strange in her ears, as if it came from a long way off.

"So," she began nervously, looking across at the tall dark haired boy with the intense, twinkling eyes. "Do you?"

He frowned. "Do I what?"

"Think that I'm crazy," she responded with a sigh. Suddenly it seemed to matter so much that this familiar stranger believed her.

Jack was quick to respond. "No, of course not. It's just such an awesome story. You mean that you actually fell into the sea and something saved you? Some kind of great invisible horse?"

Grace shrugged. "My mom says that I must have had a concussion and just imagined it all."

"And do you believe her?"

"I try to, but…"

"But not deep down," finished Jack."

Grace twirled her mug around in her fingers. "I don't know," she admitted.

"And then of course there's the weird link between your horse's name and the stud here," he reminded her. "Heathwaite horses were known all over the country at one time. Your Magic must be a descendent, I suppose.

There are so many coincidences, it's weird, and I'm sure that I *have* heard something about an old legend. My gran will know."

"Your gran will know what?" came a lilting voice from the half open back door.

Grace's eyes opened wide with surprise when an elderly, white haired lady marched into the room.

"Ah," she exclaimed, raising her eyebrows. "The young lady with the lovely horse."

"Mrs. Jenkins!" gasped Grace. "*You're* Jack's gran?"

When the old lady smiled, nodding her head in response, her translucent skin crinkled into a thousand tiny lines. Her twinkling eyes, however, were as bright as her grandson's.

"Call me Mollie," she insisted. "Everyone else does. *Mrs. Jenkins* makes me sound old."

"But I thought you lived in a cottage near the shore. I mean…This is weird. First you saved Magic and now your grandson has saved me…"

"Actually," cut in Jack, "technically it was Buster who saved you. And what do you mean, my gran saved Magic?"

"It was just fate, I suppose," continued Mollie, ignoring him. "Being in the right place at the right time. Life is sometimes like that, you know… Now, young man."

Turning away, she looked pointedly at Jack. "Why don't you pour me some hot chocolate while your young friend tells me all about it."

For the second time that day Grace unburdened herself, telling her tale hurriedly and leaving nothing out.

"And you have kept all this to yourself?" remarked Mollie when she finally finished.

"Well… not exactly. I tried to tell my mom some of it, but she just thinks I had a concussion, and I told Nell, a friend of mine from school. Nell told me about this place, actually. Well, at least, her mom told her and she told me, but she couldn't come here with me."

"Steady now," smiled Mollie. "What did this 'Nell's mom' actually tell you about Heathwaite Hall?"

"Just that it had the same name as my Magic and it used to be a stud… And she said that there was a legend or something," she remembered, her voice rising with excitement. "And Jack…" She looked across to where he was perched on the edge of the range. "You said that, too… about a legend."

"Well, there is a legend," remarked Mollie. "But before I tell you about it, I want you to come and see something."

Grace dutifully stood up, her mind in a whirl. Suddenly she felt that at last she was about to get some answers. The thought both thrilled and terrified her.

CHAPTER nine

Mollie led the way along a dark, high-ceilinged corridor where wood paneling covered the walls and long gone faces stared down at them with squinty eyes.

"Our ancestors," she announced proudly with a flourish of her hand. With the other she pushed open a heavy oak door to reveal a large square room with huge windows. The sun shone in from the garden beyond and Grace gasped.

"It's lovely," she exclaimed, looking eagerly around to see horses everywhere. Beautiful paintings graced every wall, all of noble looking Thoroughbreds with flowing manes and tails.

"This," announced Mollie, stopping in front of a tall, marble fireplace, "is Heathwaite Magic Moment."

"Magic," breathed Grace. "My Magic. They look just the same."

"Told you so," laughed Jack.

"Many, many years ago," began Mollie, "the best Thoroughbreds in the country were bred here, at Heathwaite Hall. My great, great grandfather Roger Cardew dedicated his whole life to the stud, but he lived alone except for his servants, and when he became sick it went downhill. His stallion man sold off some of the good mares and ran off with the money. His best stallion, Heathwaite Tempest, broke its leg and the only other really well bred sire proved to be impotent. When the stud lost its reputation it broke his heart and, in desperation, he traveled the length and breadth of the country, searching for a suitable stallion to retrieve its good name… That stallion was named Spirit… Come, I'll show you his picture."

Dutifully Grace followed her back along the tall dark corridor and into the imposing entrance hall, followed by Buster, who seemed to have made her his own personal property, and Jack, whose pleasant, suntanned face appeared to wear a permanent smile.

A wide staircase with an ornate wooden balustrade curved up from the large square hallway. Grace peered up to see more horses gracing the dark walls and, where the stairs turned, staring down at them through huge shining eyes, was the most magnificent horse she had ever seen.

"Spirit," announced Mollie proudly. A heavy silence fell between them as they took in the stallion's proud stance.

"He looks as if he is about to jump right out of the painting," breathed Grace. "Did he save the stud?"

Mollie shook her head sadly. "Come back into the kitchen and I'll tell you the rest if the story."

"There was one good filly left," she began once they were settled next to the comforting warmth of the range.

Grace shivered, despite the heat, suddenly afraid of what Mollie was about to tell her.

"There was one good filly left, Heathwaite Magic Moment, and the stallion bonded with her at once. They were totally inseparable. Roger Cardew's health had deteriorated, but he was obsessed by the desire to see their first foal born; the foal that was to bring back the stud's good name. It is said that he used to sit in the drawing room window all day long, just watching the two horses graze in the meadow in front of the house, waiting for spring when the foal would be born.

"It was March when it all went wrong. The filly was halfway down the meadow and Spirit had wandered off to the water trough when a pack of dogs from the village appeared. They raced toward her, and when she galloped off they followed in frenzy, barking and snapping at her heels. Sprit galloped down the slope after them, ears flat back and teeth bared, but he was too late. She fell from the cliff before he could reach her. And he…"

Mollie turned and looked at Grace, tears glistening in her bright eyes. "He leaped straight off the cliff after her. They say his hoof prints are there still, but I have never seen them."

Grace heard the clock ticking loudly in the silence and a pain flooded her heart. "So they both died."

"No, that's just it," announced Mollie. "That is the real tragedy. The filly got caught on a ledge ten feet down the cliff face. They eventually managed to haul her up but she lost the foal she was carrying. Roger Cardew died that night. They say it was a heart attack, but I believe that his heart was just broken."

"And the legend?" asked Grace. Mollie looked at her for a moment, as if unsure of whether or not to go on.

"Please…" whispered Grace.

"It is said that the mighty stallion lives on," she said quietly. "He has been sighted many times over the years, searching the sea and coastline for the filly he loved and the future he lost. It is said that he will never rest until his line lives on again."

Grace looked across at Jack, heart thumping. "Now do you believe me?" she whispered.

"Look," Mollie said as she stood up and went across to the sink, busying herself with everyday things, "it's just an old legend. There are hundreds of stories like it along this coast, so don't you go scaring yourself. Your mother is right, I'm sure; you were half drowned and had probably hit your head when you imagined the great horse that saved you. And as for your Magic acting up as she has been, well, what youngster wouldn't get spooked at times?"

"So you really don't believe in the Spirit of the Sea?" asked Grace, looking at Mollie with a puzzled frown. She was just so confused.

"No." The old lady turned away, plunging her hands into the sink. "So be a bit more careful about where you ride that nervous filly of yours until she's had a bit more experience, and you will be fine, I'm sure."

"Yes," agreed Jack. "And stay away from the cliff top. Come on, I'll walk part way home with you."

He stood up, stretching his arms above his head and calling for Buster, who ran around in excitement chasing his tail. Grace hung back when he went out into the yard, sensing the doubt in Mollie's denial and wanting to ask her one last time.

"So you *really* don't believe it?" Her fingers closed around the old lady's arm, noting its frailty through the thin stuff of her blouse as she waited for her answer.

"No."

Mollie caught her eye and then glanced away uneasily.

"It *can't* be true," she murmured, covering Grace's hand with her own. "Things like that don't really happen. Forget the legend of the sea spirit, my dear. Stay away from the shore and get on with your life."

"But I don't think I can," responded Grace.

Mollie looked back at her then, her bright eyes shadowed with concern. She nodded gently letting out a sigh. "Then be very, very careful," she advised.

"I know another route, if you're worried," suggested Jack as Grace tightened her girth and swung into the saddle. "There's a bridle path at the back of the house that comes out near the village. You wouldn't need to go near the cliff top if you went that way."

Grace hesitated, wanting to say that she wasn't afraid of riding along the cliff top path and then remembering that headlong gallop toward her doom.

"So you do believe the legend, then?" They hadn't spoken of it until that moment, and now suddenly it stood between them. As Grace pondered the question, the answer came at once; she had to find out the truth... for Magic's sake.

Jack shrugged. "You heard what my gran said."

"Yes," responded Grace. "And I saw her face too...

Look, believe what you like, but I know that there's something out there, and I intend to find out what it is."

"So," remarked Jack. "How are we going to do that?"

At the word *we* Grace's expression brightened. Relief flooded over her "You'll help me, then?"

He splayed his hands, reaching down to grab a stick from beneath the huge oak tree that stretched its massive boughs protectively above them; just as it must have done when Spirit and his silver filly walked this way all those years ago, Grace realized with a sense of awe.

"I suppose someone has to," grinned Jack, hurling the stick as hard as he could. As Buster raced off after it her mind snapped sharply back to now.

"Well, let's start by looking for the hoof prints tomorrow," she suggested eagerly. "I don't know what good it will do but it's a start."

"And then we'll have to find a way to –"

"Let's just find the hoof prints first," cut in Grace.

"Well if you're riding here, then don't use the cliff top path," advised Jack. "Or better still, I'll meet you halfway."

"Thank you," she replied with relief, thinking how great it was to finally have the support of someone who actually believed her.

Sue was home when Grace burst into the kitchen. Grace longed to share the events of the day, but she wasn't sure if she should tell her mother about it. Her mother took a casserole out of the oven, her pretty face pink and shiny with the heat.

"I've made your favorite, hon," she called. "And I've got a DVD for us to watch later. Your father is coming over too. It's called *The Horse Whisperer*. You'll love it."

"I've read the book," said Grace. "It's terrific."

"Well, then," remarked Sue. "we'll be like a real family again… just for tonight, though, so don't go counting on it."

Grace could hardly contain her excitement and suddenly the traumatic events of the day slipped into second place. "Does that mean that you've forgiven him?" she asked eagerly.

"I's early to say, I'm afraid," sighed her mother. "But at least it's a start."

As they ate their supper, side by side at the kitchen table, Grace waited for the right moment to relate her experiences. *Today Magic almost galloped off the cliff with me, but a boy and his dog saved me. And I found out from his grandmother that there really is a horse spirit that haunts the coastline…*

No, she cut off her thoughts right there. If she told her mother that now, it would only worry her and spoil the whole evening. She would tell her tomorrow, after she and Jack went to search for the hoof prints.

The film proved to be every bit a good as Grace had hoped, especially with both her parents beside her. Things were really looking up, she decided.

After popcorn, and a conversation about the movie, she and her mother walked her dad back to his car, laughing, joking and talking about the film. For Grace it seemed like the old times that she had thought to be long gone.

When her father's car disappeared into the darkness of the night her mother wandered off to bed as if in a daze, but Grace stayed downstairs for a while, staring out into the night to see twinkling lights way out across the ocean. How had she actually managed to put spirit horses and near death experiences to the back of her mind for a while, she wondered?

The memories rushed in as she went out to check on Magic, and all her insecurities flooded back.

She fought them off with a determined smile. *You have to stop being so pathetic,* she told herself. Her comments floated off unannounced into the soft night air, and she took a breath. "Life is for living," she announced determinedly.

Grace had turned the outside light on and taken the precaution of closing Magic's top door before she left her earlier. The filly nickered as soon as her girl slid the resistant bolt, blowing gently through her nostrils; a pale silvery shape in the gloom of the night.

Grace heaved a sigh of relief. "Everything is going to be fine, girl," she whispered against the warmth of her horse's velvety nose, suddenly believing it. Wait until she told Nell about the meeting with Jack Jenkins, she thought; she would be green with envy.

She closed the door again, and as she switched off the light the moon rose high in the sky, giving the whole world a magical silvery glow. She hurried back to the soft warm lights of the cottage, feeling better that she had in days.

Her positive mood still lingered next morning, when she woke to see sunlight streaming through her window and remembered about Jack and his huge gray dog. She leaped out of bed, quickly washed and dressed, and then raced downstairs two steps at a time.

"You're in a hurry," remarked her mother. She was

sitting in the kitchen sipping tea from her favorite blue and white china mug. "Want some breakfast?"

Grace glanced at her watch. "Just toast, please… but I can make it."

"No," Sue shook her head firmly. "For once I don't have to go to work, so the least I can do is make my favorite daughter some toast."

"I'm your only daughter," smiled Grace, heating the teakettle.

It was later than she intended by the time she mounted up and set off along the road at a brisk trot. Jack would be waiting already, by the oak tree where they had arranged to meet at ten o'clock. She and her mother had gotten so carried away talking about *The Horse Whisperer* that she had lost track of the time.

"Come on, girl," she said, turning Magic away from the lane onto a narrow trail.

The silver filly balked, trying to move toward the cliff top. "Don't start now," Grace said crossly, slapping her neck with the end of the reins. "You're afraid of the sea, so why do you want to go there now?" Magic lowered her head and reluctantly did her girl's bidding, snatching at a branch as Grace leaned down to open the wicket gate that let into the wood.

True to his word, Jack was waiting when they reached the huge oak tree in the meadow beyond the cluster of trees. Buster barked happily, racing around them in circles and they set off side by side across the grass. Grace stole a glance at Jack to find that he was looking at her, too, and her cheeks turned a fiery pink.

98

"So where shall we start?" she mumbled nervously.

He grinned, teeth flashing white against the golden tan of his skin. "At the beginning," he suggested cheekily, and suddenly she was laughing, too. It seemed ridiculous that they could feel so light-hearted when they both faced such an awesome task as defending their future and trying to track down an ancient spirit.

Of course, it seemed like a joke … but it wasn't a joke, was it? Still, maybe it was, and maybe the joke had been on her the whole time, firing up her imagination.

Half an hour later Magic was settled once again in the stallion box with a net of hay. Grace and Jack set off side-by-side toward the cliff top, crossing the meadow beyond the hall, their feet soundless on the springy turf. Grace stared out toward the ocean, drawing back from the perilous drop of the cliff face, her heart flipping over as she imagined the brave stallion, leaping to his doom after the mare he loved.

"Of course, if the hoof prints *are* still there, then wouldn't they just be here in this meadow?" she asked tentatively. "I mean, surely, this must be where Spirit jumped."

"But why hasn't my gran ever seen them then?" responded Jack.

"Maybe she's never really looked," suggested Grace, scouring the ground for traces of hoof prints."

After half an hour of searching, when they had reached the end of the open meadow and set off back along the pathway again, Jack suddenly stopped.

"Look," he announced, throwing a stick for Buster, "this is crazy. Just stop and think about it. We're looking for the hoof prints of an unshod horse that jumped off a cliff over a hundred years ago."

Grace giggled. Suddenly sea spirits seemed a million miles away. "Well, I suppose… if you put it like that," she agreed.

"Come on." Jack turned determinedly on his heel. "Let's just go back. Maybe we can find a book about the legend, or take a look on the Internet."

They were halfway across the meadow when, with a rush of delight, Grace suddenly saw them; daisies growing near the edge of the cliff in two perfect arcs on the ground. For a moment her heart seemed to stand still.

"Look," she whispered. "I think that maybe we were looking for the wrong thing."

Jack crouched down, running his fingers gently across the delicate flowers. "Do you really think that this is what they mean?" he asked, looking up at Grace.

When she saw the expression on his face she realized that he believed it too. Her breath caught in her throat and her mouth turned dry. "I think so," she croaked, nodding her head madly.

The wind whipped up, flipping her shiny dark hair across her face. Was that a distant, awesome cry?

His fingers closed tightly around her arm. "Let's get out of here," he suggested, taking hold of her hand. Grace was only too eager to take his suggestion. They didn't notice Buster, hanging back, staring out to sea with a whine deep down in his throat before bounding after them as though the hounds were on his tail.

CHAPTER TEN

"So what now?" asked Grace. They were back in the large kitchen at Heathwaite Hall, both subdued and thoughtfully sipping hot chocolate. Neither of them had spoken of their experiences on the cliff top until Jack had carefully boiled water and made the drinks, restoring a sense of normality before examining their hidden demons.

Eventually he shrugged, placing his yellow flowered mug firmly down onto the table. "The question is," he announced. "Do we really believe it? Have we actually found the mystical hoof prints… or… are we just spooking ourselves?" Buster padded across the room to rest his huge head on Grace's knee. She rubbed the backs of his ears absentmindedly, thoughts racing inside her head.

"The daisies *could* have grown in the place where Spirit's hooves left the ground, I suppose," she began.

Suddenly Jack grinned. "And pigs might fly," he chortled. "Anyway, they're not there now."

Grace looked across at him with a puzzled frown and for a moment he held her gaze, his eyes sparkling with merriment.

"Here," he eventually announced with a flourish, holding out a slightly limp looking bunch of daisies. For a moment time seemed suspended as they both stared at the tiny flowers. Grace was the first to move.

"Jack," she cried. "What have you done? At least put them in water." She leaped from her seat, grabbed a glass from the side and filled it with tap water before holding it out to him.

Reverently he lowered in the delicate blooms, his tanned face suddenly turning pale. "I shouldn't have done it, should I?" he murmured.

Grace shrugged. "Well, I thought that at first, but then again, why not? They're just flowers, after all… aren't they?"

"Of course they are," he announced, his good humor restored. "And we're being ridiculous."

"Do you know," agreed Grace. "I do believe you're right."

Mollie appeared just then clutching a canvas bag. She placed it down onto the table and sat heavily. "I think I'm getting too old to help out at the day care center," she announced. "In fact, to be honest, I think that it's almost time for them be looking after me. Be a good lad, Jack, and make your old gran a cup of tea."

As he jumped up she reached across to pick up the small glass of daisies. "It's very nice of the two of you to bring me flowers," she said smiling, "but you might have picked living ones."

Grace peered over her shoulder and a kind of sadness loomed inside her when she saw that the bright little blooms had now drooped completely. Was it a sign, she wondered? No, she had to stop these crazy thoughts. They were just flowers.

"We'll pick you some more," she quickly offered.

Mollie raised her hand. "No, leave them where they are. Flowers are meant to feel the rays of the sun, not to wilt away in the gloom. Oh, and by the way," She looked eagerly across at Grace, "I met someone who knows you today… well, knows *of* you, that is."

"Knows *me*?" echoed Grace.

"Yes," responded Mollie. "A handicapped lady named Mary Gibson, mother of your friend, Nell, I believe?"

"Oh yes," said Grace. "Nell goes to school with me, and you wouldn't believe what a great person she is. She spends all her spare time looking after her mom."

"Well, Mary is a lovely woman, too," remarked Mollie. "And so brave. I think she had a stroke a couple of years ago. It must be tough for her daughter, though. I'll call in on them one of these days when I'm out that way."

Jack handed over her cup of tea then and she took it gratefully, sipping the steaming liquid with satisfaction.

"Come on, Grace," he urged. "I'll show you around the house. See you later, Gran."

"Thanks, love," she responded, relaxing back into her rocking chair.

"I felt really bad when my gran said that about the flowers" admitted Jack. He and Grace had spent an hour or so going through the extensive library at Heathwaite for any information on the legend of the spirit horse, to no avail. Now he was walking alongside Magic as she made her way homewards.

"She's right though, isn't she," she remarked. "Flowers do look better growing."

"I don't really know why I picked them," he responded. "To retaliate, I suppose. It just seemed such a scary thought that they might be Spirit's hoof prints." For a few moments the only sound to break the languid silence of the sunny afternoon was the gentle thud of Magic's hooves on the grassy trail.

"Well, I'll be back at school tomorrow," Grace eventually remarked. "So I'll ask Nell how her mom found out about the legend. She might know where we can find a book about it. I can't believe that there wasn't one in your library. You seem to have everything else. Anyway…" She looked down at Jack's shiny dark head curiously. "Why aren't you at school?"

He shrugged, glancing quickly up at her and then reaching down to pick up a stick for Buster. "My parents are working abroad, so I had to come and live with Gran for a while. It was too late to get into a normal school this term so I have a tutor who comes to the house."

"How fancy," remarked Grace. "How much longer are you here, anyway?" Suddenly his answer seemed very important.

"A few more weeks," he replied and her heart did a funny little flip.

"I'll come again on Saturday," she told him, nodding her head. "Unless I find anything else, out of course. If I do I'll come after school. Do you have a cell phone?"

Jack made a face. "That's a sore point. My dad promised to get me one before they went away and he never got around to it. I can't expect Gran to fork out for it and I have no money, well not enough to buy a phone anyway. Tell you what…"

He hurled the stick for Buster, who raced off after it and then rummaged in his pocket to produce a slip of crumpled paper. "There," he announced, scribbling down a number with a stump of chewed pen. He thrust it toward her, suddenly awkward. "This is the house number. Call if you find out anything at all and I'll come to you."

Grace left him half an hour later, standing by the huge oak tree with his fingers curled around Buster's collar. It made her feel a whole lot better to know that he was there, believing in her. She waved and he waved back, their eyes connecting across the distance.

"Don't forget to call," he shouted as she and Magic rounded the corner onto the lane.

Both her parents were in the kitchen at Sea View when she burst in carrying her tack.

"What are you doing with that in here?" asked her mother.

"Cleaning it," she replied with a grin.

Her father nodded wisely. "For the riding club show on Saturday, I suppose?"

Grace's stomach churned and ice filled her veins. She couldn't believe it was this weekend, and she hadn't even been practicing.

"No!" Her exclamation took both her parents by surprise. "Isn't it next month?"

"Go and get the schedule," suggested her father and she raced off to check. Sure enough, there it was: "RIDING CLUB SPRING SHOW, March 29th."

Grace held the paper out before her as if expecting the words to change. "But I can't," she wailed.

Todd stood tall, broadening his six-foot frame. "Grace Melrose," he announced. "How many times have I told you, there is no such word as can't in the Melrose family?"

"You are a fine one to talk," grumbled Sue. "If she's worried about it, then as far as I'm concerned she doesn't have to go."

"No," Grace placed her saddle and bridle carefully down onto the floor, replying with far more confidence than she was feeling. "Dad's right, it'll be fine."

"See," he announced proudly, "I knew she wasn't a quitter." When Sue threw him a disparaging glance, he had the sense to blush.

When Grace set off for school the next morning gray clouds hid the sun and drizzle ran down the back of her neck. She felt as if the weather had come out in sympathy with her, reflecting her mood; suddenly it all just seemed too much. The scares with Magic, her fears about the spirit horse, and then those daisy shapes on the cliff top. She couldn't get the story out of her head, imagining the valiant stallion again and again, leaping to his doom after the filly he loved. Sometimes she felt as if the whole thing was totally ridiculous and sometimes, like now, it seemed so real that she wanted to just run away. At least today she could talk to Nell. Nell was so sensible and down to earth; she would know what to do.

But then again, what *could* she do? What could anybody do? Even if they found a book that told of the legend then it wouldn't necessarily spell out for them how to keep the great stallion, Spirit, at bay. And that was what she wanted, wasn't it? To keep Magic safe from the threat that hung over her... or was there a threat at all? Was it just her own stupid imagination working overtime?

Maybe the show was a good thing. At least, that's what Jack had said when she called him the night before. "It'll give you something else to focus on," he told her. "And I'll come with you."

After the phone clicked down she had just sat for a moment, thinking about him. How could someone you only just met become an integral part of your life? She felt as if she had known him forever.

"Boyfriend?" her mother had remarked with a teasing smile.

"Just a friend," she quickly responded, squirming inside. Was he her boyfriend? The idea had sat comfortably as she carefully soaped Magic's saddle, thinking about the next day and Saturday. It just felt as if everything was happening too fast, like a roller coaster ride with no way to get off.

Later that morning, in first break, Nell and Grace were sitting in the school cloakroom. After listening avidly while Grace related yesterday's adventure, Nell stared at her, her gray eyes wide with excitement.

"Why doesn't anything like that ever happen to me?" she cried.

Grace grimaced. "Do you really want to almost gallop off a cliff and be scared silly all day?" she exclaimed.

Nell shrugged. "Of course not, it's just that… oh, nothing. I'll ask my mom if she knows where there's a book on local legends as soon as I get home, but I think you're right. It might not be any help at all."

"Well, there's nothing on the Internet about it," remarked Grace. "Jack and I spent ages looking yesterday and we have to try and do something."

"But what do you think might happen if you don't get rid of this spirit horse?" asked Nell.

For a moment, Grace went quiet. "Maybe nothing… or maybe Magic will just get crazier and crazier every time she thinks he's near."

"Does Jack believe it?"

"I think so," Grace looked down at the ground. "At least he says he does."

Nell twisted her hands together, flicking back her long blonde curly hair. "Tell me again about him," she begged. "Is he tall or short… and is he good looking?"

Grace conjured up an image of Jack's suntanned face, his dark eyes twinkling like stars from beneath a thatch of glossy black hair.

"Oh yes," she announced, feeling suddenly awkward. "He is… I suppose. Anyway, he's coming to the show on Saturday, so why don't you come along too? Then you can meet him and judge for yourself."

"I'll see," responded Nell with a sigh.

Suddenly Grace felt guilty. It felt as if everything was

about her, and that wasn't right when poor Nell's entire life was spent caring for her mom. "How *is* your mom?" she asked, genuinely wanting to know.

Nell smiled. "She's great. You have to come and meet her some day. You'd love her. Everyone does."

"And is there really no one who could look after her sometimes, you know, just to give you a break?"

"I don't mind," insisted Nell, too quickly.

Suddenly an idea began to form in Grace's mind; maybe there was a way that she could help her friend.

As soon as Grace got home that evening, she quickly changed and raced out to the stable yard where Magic waited impatiently, tossing her head and whinnying. Grace slipped on her head collar and fed her an apple she had sneaked from the bowl in the house, before going to get out her grooming kit.

"I'll feed you when we've finished," she promised. "After all, you've been guzzling silage all day."

Magic crunched happily on the apple as Grace set to work with a body brush and curry comb, enjoying the effort. "I hope you haven't forgotten all the work we did," she remarked as she slid the bridle over her ears. The filly obligingly opened her mouth and Grace buckled up the throatlatch and fastened the noseband. If Magic behaved, then maybe there would still be time to ride over to see Jack this evening, and maybe even put her plan for Nell into action.

To her relief, the silver gray filly seemed calm and relaxed, much more like her old self. As she worked some circles and headed for the first fence Grace's fears disappeared and her heart began to soar. Magic was totally supple and obedient, her canter rhythmic and impulsive, a real show jumping canter. She felt the stride, meeting every fence perfectly, confidence soaring.

So concentrated were their efforts that she didn't notice someone watching from the gate onto the road until she finally reined in and allowed Magic to stretch. Steam rose in gentle clouds and Grace's cheeks were pink with both effort and elation.

"That was great."

At the sound of Jack's voice, a funny feeling wriggled inside her and she turned toward him, heart racing. "Thanks," she replied. "She was good, wasn't she?"

"And so were you," he responded, his dark eyes shining with admiration.

Grace felt as if the whole world was sitting in the palm of her hand. She slipped to the ground and led Magic across to where he was perched on the fence.

"Maybe the show won't be such a disaster after all," she grinned. "Come on, help me put her away and I'll show you my house. It's not as grand as yours, though, I'm afraid."

"So this is Jack," remarked her mother when they burst into the sunny kitchen of Sea View cottage twenty minutes later. She was setting the table for two, Grace noticed; that meant that her father wasn't coming over tonight. Would they ever really get back together?

"Is he staying for dinner?" asked Sue, staring intently at the tall, dark-haired boy.

"No," he muttered turning a deep shade of red. "Thanks. My gran will be expecting me."

"Well, you're welcome anytime," responded Sue with a smile.

Grace plucked at his sleeve. "Come on, let's go outside for a while. When will dinner be, Mom?"

Her mother shooed them off. "Go on, I'll shout when it's ready."

They sat side by side on the garden wall in the evening sun, staring out toward the sparkling horizon and breathing in the aroma of the sea as they discussed all the events of the last couple of days.

"There is one thing I haven't told you," admitted Jack when he eventually stood up to leave.

Something inside Grace tightened.

"I biked along the cliff top to get here…"

"And…?" she responded.

He held her gaze for a moment and then glanced away. "And the daisies are back."

"But…" Grace looked at him doubtfully. "They can't be."

"Well…" Jack shrugged. "I am afraid that they are, just like before. Two perfect hoof prints."

"Well, let's hope that Nell's mom knows where we can get hold of a book," remarked Grace. "It might tell us something."

"It's *what* it might tell us that worries me," he admitted. "Sometimes I think that my gran knows more than she's letting on."

When he saw Grace's horrified expression, he grinned.

"Pay no attention to me. The past can't hurt you, you know, and I probably just didn't actually pick all the daisies anyway."

"Well, why didn't you say that?" she exclaimed, thumping him on the shoulder.

When Buster joined forces with her, leaping up onto Jack's back, he pushed them both off.

"Hey…! Quit bullying," he laughed, grabbing Buster's collar. "And whose side are you on, anyway?" The huge dog rewarded him with a wet lick down his face and Jack pushed him down.

"Come on, boy, time to go home," he said, reaching for his bicycle. "See you tomorrow, Grace."

"Yes…" For a moment she hesitated. "I'll come over to your place though, if that's all right? There's something I need to ask your grandmother."

Jack stopped, looking back at her, one hand shading his eyes from the crimson light of the setting sun. "Now what would you have to ask my gran about?" he asked curiously.

Grace raised her eyebrows. "Wait and see," she told him.

CHAPTER ELEVEN

The moon was high in the sky by the time Grace went to check on Magic for the last time that evening. Its silver light shone so bright that she didn't even need a flashlight to make her way along the pathway that led into the small stable yard.

The outside light shone down on the cobblestones, warm and yellow. "I think that maybe everything's going to be OK now, girl," she told the inquisitive filly, her hand on the top door. Should she shut it? It seemed such a shame to keep poor Magic in darkness. For a moment more she hesitated before pushing it firmly and sliding the bolt.

"Sorry girl," she called. "Better safe than sorry." But then again, what could possibly happen, she asked herself as she hurried back into the house. Magic could hardly get out over the half-door. Tomorrow night she would leave it open.

＊ ＊ ＊ ＊ ＊

She wasn't sure what it was that woke her a few hours later. A distant banging maybe, or was it the thud of galloping hooves. Dreams and reality seemed melded into one as she opened her eyes in the half-light.

"Grace…Grace!" Was that her mother's voice she could hear? Sleep slipped away and she sat bolt upright; it wasn't a dream, the sounds were real.

Her mother's voice came again, sharp and urgent. "I think Magic's out." She appeared on the landing tying the belt on her silk robe. "Quick… come on."

Grace pushed her feet into her slippers and raced downstairs two steps at a time, grabbing a jacket to cover her pajamas as she struggled with the back door bolt. Her mother was right behind her as she raced along the pathway. Her heart was somewhere in her boots.

Suddenly she stopped, staring through the murky dawn light at the stable door. It was closed, just as she had left it. A wave of relief left her struggling for breath.

"Look!" cried her mother. "You were right all the time. There is a horse stalking you, but it's definitely no ghost or wandering spirit. It must have gotten loose from somewhere and come looking for Magic. Is she in heat? Maybe it's a stallion who's come looking for a mate?"

Grace stared at the marks on the wooden door, the scrapes that could only be made by teeth and the half rounded indentations. Behind it Magic nickered loudly and she rushed to slide back the bolt. Her head appeared, wide-eyed and nervous.

"You poor girl," cried Sue. "Were you frightened by the horrid horse?"

Grace flicked on the light, staring at the filly's expression. It wasn't fear she saw in her shining dark eyes. Her heart turned cold as she ran her hand down the silvery softness of her nose. *What if the horse was…?* No, she couldn't even begin to let herself think that.

"We'll call the police and report it," suggested her mother. "And don't worry; obviously she's safe enough for now. Maybe I should call that farmer at the end of the lane… what's his name?"

"Mr. Robins," replied Grace automatically.

"He's sure to know who owns a stallion around these parts. Come on, it's only five a.m., there's time for another hour in bed."

Grace looked at her vacantly. Bed… how could she even think of going back to bed after… after what? After a loose horse had come searching for Magic, that's what. It couldn't get to her because the stable door was closed. But how had it gotten past the gate from the lane?

"Come on," urged her mother. "It's cold out here."

Grace looked at Magic one last time before flicking off the light and carefully closing the top door again. Magic didn't look afraid. She looked nervous and excited and very, very alive. The thoughts that had been pounding around in Grace's brain since she first saw the marks on the stable door culminated into a sudden, certain knowledge. The Spirit of the Sea had come looking for his mate. He knew… he knew that Magic was the descendant of the mare he had given his life for. But who would ever believe her… except maybe Jack?

The house was silent, with only the ticking of the clock

in the hallway to break its hush. How soon could she go to see Jack, wondered Grace, looking at the small green figures on the clock beside her bed. Five thirty. She could hardly go there now, could she? And what about school?

She jumped out of bed and padded along the landing, peeping around her mother's door to hear her rhythmic breathing. Maybe she could get there and back before she woke. No, it was too far. So when, when could she talk to him? Her head felt as if it was whirling around in crazy circles. Spirit had come looking for Magic. The more she thought of it the more sure she became, but she had no one to tell. And what if he got to her... really got to her? She had to see Jack... and then what? Fear dragged her down.

By seven o'clock she had fed and mucked out Magic's stall, carefully fastening the bolt on her half door and fitting a padlock that she found in the kitchen drawer. Even a spirit horse couldn't open a padlock. She looked over the door one last time. "If only you could talk, girl."

The filly tossed her head, nickering under her breath and Grace felt a pain in the region of her heart.

"Don't worry, girl," she promised. "I'll make sure that the horrid stallion doesn't get you."

Magic's big dark eyes seemed to stare beyond her, into the distance, as if seeing something that Grace could not. Suddenly Grace was filled with dread. Did her precious horse really want to be saved?

Checking the lock again, she hurried back into the house to find her mother about to leave for work already. "Come on, hon," she urged impatiently. "You're going to be late for the bus." Grace reached up to kiss her soft, warm cheek, inhaling the aroma of her favorite perfume.

"You OK?" her mother asked. Grace felt tears pressing against the backs of her eyes and she glanced away, too late. Sue placed a gentle hand on her shoulder, turning her around so that she could look into her face. The tears forced an entry, squeezing from between her tightly shut lids.

"Surely you're not still worrying about spirit horses!" she exclaimed, hugging her daughter tightly. Suddenly Grace felt five years old again, closeted in that warm safe place where someone else faces your fears for you. The trickle of tears became a flood.

"What if it was him, Spirit I mean, come to take Magic?"

"Grace!" Her mother's firm response stopped her tears. "Think about it… Since when could ghosts or spirits leave marks on doors? There is an old legend, I know, but that is all it is… just a legend. Can't you see? You've let it grow totally out of proportion, and this episode with Magic last night just proves that. She's a filly, it's spring and somewhere near here there is a stallion that's been calling to her. Now it's escaped and come looking for a mate. It's nature, that's all, pure and simple. You don't need to be worried about legends any more for now; we have proof that this particular stallion is real. I'll call around as soon as I get to work and see if I can find out where it came from, and in the meantime, just keep her door firmly shut and bolted."

Sue took her daughter by the shoulders, looking earnestly into her face, willing her to believe it. Taking comfort from her mother's confidence, Grace felt her certainty weaken. Could it be really be true? Had she been overreacting all this time? But what about Nell and Jack? They believed it too… or did they? Maybe they were just humoring her.

"So no more silly ideas!" Her mother gave her a last quick hug, wiping the tearstains from beneath her eyes with her thumbs, as if she were a little girl again.

Grace lowered her head. "No," she mumbled. "No more silly ideas."

"Promise?"

She held her mother's gaze, feeling better than she had in ages. "Promise."

During their first break Grace got Nell on her own and she poured out her story, hardly stopping for breath until she had relieved herself of every tiny detail. Now she waited with bated breath for her friend's response, watching the expression on her broad face with a kind of fluttery feeling in her stomach.

Her mother's advice had been going around and around inside her head all morning and she waited for the questions that Nell was sure to pose:

But what about Magic almost galloping off the cliff and going crazy on the shore and behaving weirdly in her stable? And what about the daisies, and the hoof prints on the sand?

It seemed to her that there were so many unanswered questions. To her surprise, Nell's reaction was just to nod, purse her lips and draw her brows into a concentrated frown.

"Well, it does make sense," she remarked.

"So you believe it, too?" Grace didn't know whether to laugh or cry.

Nell shrugged. "Well, as your mom said, it's spring. Magic *could* just be infatuated with some local stallion. Horses have strong instincts at this time of year."

"But what about all the other things?" asked Grace. "The way she's been behaving and the hoof prints and the daisies…?"

"Look," sensible as ever, Nell leaned toward her friend, "I see where you're coming from, but it could all point to the same thing. She could have sensed that he was around, maybe even heard him call. After all, her ears are much more finely tuned than ours… and, if you really stop to think about it, our ideas about a great spirit horse coming from the sea were a little nuts, I suppose."

"Well, at least you said *our* ideas," grumbled Grace.

Nell smiled. "Well, they were our ideas; I believed it every bit as much as you did, but I'd rather believe there's another explanation."

Suddenly Grace's expression brightened. "Well, if you put it like that," she agreed, feeling as if a great weight was being lifted from her shoulders. "What do you think Jack will say?"

"Same as I did, I bet," responded Nell. "Come on, it's almost time for class and I have to get some books from my locker."

As soon as she got home, Grace raced around the side of the house to see Magic. The silver filly pricked her ears and moved toward the half door, pushing her head into her owner's chest.

"Do you really have a boyfriend, girl?" smiled Grace, glancing nervously around. "Well don't you worry, there's no stallion going to get you while I'm around… but then again…" She looked earnestly into her horse's dark shining eyes. "… maybe you want him to get you."

Knowing that she really should get in some practice for the show before she set off, Grace nevertheless found herself riding *past* the paddock with the brightly colored obstacles and heading off along the lane toward Heathwaite Hall. She had to see Jack, had to run their ideas past him. What if he totally disbelieved it?

Staring out across the crystal sea she remembered the day when it all began. The feel of the wind in her face as Magic stretched out along the smooth sweep of the shore; the moment when she saw the hoof prints. Time had seemed momentarily suspended as Magic suddenly plunged beneath her. Then had come the hard shock of the sand followed by a swell of horror as she galloped away, her tail held out behind her like a silver banner.

Had something really saved Grace when she fell into the waves, or *was* it just her imagination? It had seemed so real at the time. With a sudden sense of urgency she picked up the reins and urged Magic into a trot. Perhaps she should have waited until her mother came home before she set off for Heathwaite Hall, or at least called her to find out if she had found out whose stallion it was. What if it was still on the loose? Turning the filly's head away from the cliff top route, she headed onto the trail that led through the trees. Maybe she should have called Jack instead of just setting off.

The wind was picking up, rustling the branches way above her head, and when Magic spooked, snorting at an invisible monster, she took a firm hold of the reins, all her old fears flooding in.

"Come on girl, don't be silly. It's just the wind."

She spoke out loud, needing to hear the sound of her own voice, staring ahead toward the light that beckoned beyond the all-encompassing woodland. It was almost within her grasp when a crashing in the undergrowth stopped Magic dead. She raised her tail and lifted her beautiful head, ears pricked toward the sound, her every muscle taut and shivering. Grace clamped her legs on, driving her forward… "Not again… please not again."

When a dark shape burst out at them for a moment her heart seemed to stand still, and then a giggle bubbled up in her throat.

"Buster!" she cried as the huge gray Irish wolfhound appeared running around the silver filly in crazy circles. Unperturbed, Magic lowered her head, snorting more gently now, and for just a moment the big dog reached up and touched noses as if in greeting.

"Look at that. Who would believe it," broke in Jack's voice.

When she saw his smiling face Grace's whole world seemed to slip back on track, all her fears forgotten.

"You two scared the life of me!" she cried. "You should have told me you were coming this way."

Jack's twinkling dark eyes found hers. "Sorry, I meant to call."

"It doesn't matter. I have so much to tell you… come on." She urged Magic into a trot. "Let's get out of the woods and I'll fill you in."

✳ ✳ ✳ ✳ ✳

"So?" she announced half an hour later. They were
sitting on a wooden bench at the side of a footpath that
led across the meadow toward Heathwaite Hall. Beside
them Buster lay panting slightly from his exertion while
Magic pulled at her reins, stretching for every available
mouthful of grass.

"Well, I suppose it makes sense," remarked Jack
slowly. "It's a little disappointing, really. I liked the idea
of the daisy hoof prints and the spirit horse of the sea."

"So you believe my mom too…?" Grace waited,
holding her breath for his answer.

"Obviously your friend Nell did."

"Like you, she said that it made sense; it's spring,
Magic was in heat… Oh, I don't know."

"In a way it's nice to have a sensible explanation."
He turned to look at her, a thoughtful expression on
his sun-tanned face for once. "Now you can focus all
your attention on the show this weekend. I'll come over
on Saturday if you like and watch you have your last
practice."

Grace felt the smile inside her swell until her whole
body was one big glow. "Thanks," she said. "That would
be great. Now come on, I need to see your grandmother,
remember."

CHAPTER TWELVE

Even the sun seemed to have come out for Grace's big day. She woke with a warm feeling inside her, a feeling that gradually settled into the top of her stomach like a flurry of tiny birds all flapping to get out.

As Grace raced along the landing her mother called, "Morning, darling." Grace stopped to peer around the bedroom door, stepping back to do a double take when her father's face appeared.

"Have you two… I mean are you…?"

"Back together," finished her mother for her. "It's early yet, but… we'll see."

Could life get any better, wondered Grace as she leaped down the stairs two at a time and ran outside, breathing in the clear fresh air. Beyond the cliffs the sea appeared to sparkle with a million tiny diamonds and way up above her gulls coasted in easy circles, their lonely cries like music to her ears. How could she have thought that a spirit horse roamed the coastline? How could she have possibly believed that he was going to take Magic? When she reached the stable yard however, she still stopped to trace her fingers over the shapes in the wood, just to be sure; the indentations that proved the stallion was real. He had never been back, thank heavens, and Magic seemed to be calmer now, but anyone could see that he *had* been here.

The silver filly thrust her head out over the door, eyes on the horizon and flared nostrils showing red.

"You all right, girl?" asked Grace, suddenly uneasy. Magic lowered her head as she slid the bolt, eager for her feed, and she felt herself relax. "Come on then," she smiled, giving her the bucket. "You eat up and I'll go and boil water. You have to look your best today, you know."

By eight o'clock Magic was gleaming white with her mane neatly braided. Grace stood back to survey her handiwork with a glow of satisfaction. "Now it's my turn," she announced, heading for the house. "And no rolling."

"You have to have something to eat," insisted her mother as Grace struggled into her show jacket.

The birds in her stomach began their fluttering again and she shook her head, fastening her buttons. "No, honestly, I couldn't possibly eat anything."

"And you're sure you are all right riding there on your own?" asked her father. "I could come with you." He had just walked into the kitchen, his hair still damp from the shower and for a moment Grace forgot about her nerves.

"It's so good to see you two back together!" she cried out.

"It's still early," remarked her mother, but her eyes were smiling as she glanced across at her husband.

Grace picked up her riding crop, fastening her hat and adjusting her hair. "Thanks, Dad, but I'll be fine. Jack is meeting me on the way anyway, so I won't be on my own. I'll see you there."

For just a moment she felt like taking off all the fancy riding gear she felt so unaccustomed to, putting on her comfortable old jodhpurs and T-shirt and just going out for a trail ride in the glorious sunshine.

"You'll be fine," promised her dad with a confident smile, and the moment was gone. Today she and Magic were going to prove that they really could do it, that all her training had not been in vain. It seemed like an awesome task.

Jack was waiting by the oak tree, sitting on a tree trunk whittling a piece of wood with Buster lounging at his feet.

"Don't worry, I've brought his lead," he announced, holding out a bedraggled piece of blue rope. "I was going to leave him at home, but he just looked so sad."

"Well don't let him loose when I'm jumping," warned Grace and suddenly the birds in her stomach were back tenfold.

"I don't know if I can do this," she groaned.

Jack grinned, picking up his bike from where he had discarded it on the ground. "Of course you can," he told her firmly. "I've watched you practice, remember… And at least it's taken your mind off spirit sea horses," he added, as they set off along the rough trail.

"That's true," agreed Grace, realizing that the thought hadn't entered her head since yesterday… well, not much anyway.

They saw the showgrounds long before they actually arrived. Colorful horse trailers were parked in higgledy-piggledy rows across the hillside ahead of them. Among them moved horses of all shapes, sizes and colors, walking, trotting and cantering in endless circles upon the vivid green carpet of grass. Grace could almost feel the tension from half a mile away. Or was it just her own nerves that brought the tingling sensation to her limbs?

"They all look so confident," she whispered to Jack as they entered the melee of movement and sounds.

"Then put on your show face and look confident too," he whispered back.

She laughed, an impulsive belly laugh that dissolved her nerves.

"Do you think that they're all pretending, too?" she giggled.

"No doubt about it," he told her solemnly. "And anyway, it's you two who are going to win."

"A clear round would be a gift and a rosette would be a bonus," she admitted with a broad grin. Suddenly things didn't seem so bad after all; at least she didn't have a spirit horse to worry about anymore.

Her class was scheduled for eleven a.m., and after dismounting for a while to give Magic a break, she tightened her girth again and went to mount just as her mother and father appeared.

They walked toward her, arm in arm, and a kind of glow filled her whole body.

Jack hung back but she beckoned him forward again. "Dad, this is Jack Jenkins," she said, eager for them to know each other. Her father grinned and held out his hand, pumping Jack's up and down furiously.

"Ah," he announced. "Grace's first boyfriend."

She blushed furiously and urged Magic into a trot, heading in the direction of the collecting ring where her embarrassment was soon forgotten by the sight of the professional looking riders practicing for her class.

"You look just as good as they do," called Jack from the fence as she trotted past. She grimaced but his words hit home, boosting her confidence again.

"Better," echoed her father from beside him, just as a familiar face came into view.

For a moment she froze. Was her perfect day to be spoiled after all? She glanced back behind her to see with relief that her mother and father had wandered off. The last thing she wanted for them today was to see Tina Chadwick with all the bad memories she invoked. She glanced at Grace and glanced away again with just the merest curl of her perfectly painted lips, turning her pretty face toward a good looking young man who was heading toward her carrying two ice creams. The way she greeted him left Grace in no doubt but that her father was definitely rid of her. Could today get any better?

It seemed that it could. As she trotted around the ring, plucking up courage to jump the practice fence, another familiar face appeared.

"Jack," she shouted, reining in. "Meet my friend, Nell."

Jack grinned broadly, his teeth flashing white against his tanned skin. "Hello, Nell," he said. "My gran made it, then."

Nell's face turned pink and Grace felt a momentary prickle of jealousy that faded into guilt when Nell smiled up at her.

"Thanks for asking her to come and look after my mom," she called. "It's just so great to be able to come and watch you. Magic is beautiful, isn't she?"

Jack made a face. "Yes," he announced, his dark eyes twinkling. "It's just a shame about her rider."

"Jack Jenkins!" exclaimed Grace.

"Oh," he exclaimed with a serious face. "So you think that you're beautiful too, do you?"

"No, I… well."

Grace turned Magic away and headed for the practice fence, nerves forgotten, concentrating all her attention on finding space in the busy collecting ring. When Magic cleared it with ease, her momentary embarrassment faded as she looked around with glee to see her two best friends watching proudly. *It was so nice to have both of them there,* she thought as she circled around in an impulsive canter to take the fence again.

She was third to go in the novice jumping class, following in the wake of two riders who had jumped perfect clear rounds. Magic shied at the first fence but Grace kicked her on, her determination overcoming the filly's nerves. She cat-jumped and Grace grabbed her mane and then they were clear and off toward the second fence.

It seemed then that suddenly Magic realized why they

were there. She headed for the red and white oxer with her ears pricked, soaring over with such power that it took Grace's breath away. By the time they reached the final fence she was gasping for air but they were clear, they really were clear. "To get a clear round would be a gift," she had told Jack. Well, it wasn't just a gift, it was the best present she had ever had!

She cantered through the exit with tears of joy in her eyes, gasping for breath as she pulled up in front of her small group of excited followers. Her legs buckled as she jumped to the ground and her father reached out to support her.

"Of course you do realize that you have to do it all over again now, don't you?" he remarked.

Her mother just hugged her, long and hard, while her two friends looked on with delight.

"Here," said Jack, thrusting a piece of carrot toward Magic. "I told you she could do it."

"Do it!" exclaimed Grace. "She is a total star."

There were eight clear rounds in the jump off and Grace was third to go. She entered the ring with far more confidence than the first time, knowing now that at least Magic would try to jump the fences, and if they had one or two down… no matter, she had already proved herself in Grace's eyes.

"Come on, girl," she murmured, wrapping her calves around the filly's heaving sides and taking up the contact. There was no wrong stride to the first fence this time; one, two, three, and they left the ground as if on wings, heading for the second in a purposeful canter.

She had decided not to race around in the hope of a rosette. "Think of the bigger picture," had been her father's advice. "After all, there will be lots of shows to go to this summer, and you don't want to teach her to be stupid by racing against the clock too early. A nice clear round's the best thing."

She cantered out of the ring having done just that with the clap of the spectators in her ears and so much joy in her heart that she thought she might explode.

"Well done," whispered Jack for her ears only, reaching up to touch her hand with his, and then her parents were there and everything was one big buzz.

It was late afternoon by the time they set off for home. A fourth place rosette fluttered on Magic's bridle and Grace kept glancing at it, unable to believe that they had actually won something in their very first competition.

"I told you it would be OK," remarked Jack. He was riding along beside her on his bicycle while Buster ran on ahead along the footpath.

"It was great, wasn't it," she sighed, the glow in her heart suffusing her whole body.

"Are you going to go again next month?" he asked, ginning.

"Just try and stop me," she exclaimed.

"You'll win next time," he declared and she giggled.

"Or make a complete mess of it. Maybe it was just beginner's luck."

"And maybe you just happen to have a brilliant horse."

"It was so nice of your gran to look after Nell's mom for a couple of hours," remarked Grace, changing the

subject. "She never gets to go anywhere. She hadn't even seen Magic until today."

Jack nodded. "She'll probably do it again for the next show if Nell wants to go."

"Will you still be here?"

Suddenly it seemed so important to Grace that he was.

He shook his head slowly. "A month… to be honest, I don't know; it depends on when my dad's job finishes. I hope so, though."

"I hope so too," said Grace quietly, looking away.

It was a long ride home through the woodland, but safer than the more direct route along the cliff top. Grace reined in where the path forked, feeling totally confident. The sun was still shining, Magic felt tired and relaxed and the sea stretched way out toward the horizon, merging with the hazy sky, smooth and calm and sparkling.

"And since there are no such things as spirit horses, I'm taking the short cut," she announced.

"Are you sure?" Jack looked at her nervously. "What if Magic gets spooked again?"

"She's too tired to get spooked," insisted Grace. "And it's time to put all our crazy imaginings behind us."

He shrugged. "I suppose… if you put it like that. Do you want me to come with you?"

"No." Her confidence surprised him. "Just stay here and watch if you like. You'll be able to see us until we round the headland and then we'll be almost home anyway."

Jack sat on his bike, watching the silver filly and her dark haired, straight backed rider set off along the cliff top. He had never met anyone quite like Grace; not just pretty but strong and brave too. He bit his lip, nerves fluttering somewhere inside his chest. Of course there was no spirit horse, just a high-strung four-year-old filly that sometimes panicked, that's all. Beside him Buster whined, ears pricked toward the horse and rider. Did he know something they didn't? For a moment Jack felt like calling to her to come back but he resisted the temptation. She would laugh tomorrow, he decided, when he told her how nervous he had been on her behalf.

The sea was a gentle swish in Grace's ears, the gulls a melody that pulled at her heartstrings. Beneath her Magic pranced a little, eager to be home, and she closed her hands on the reins.

"You are a star," she told her, leaning forwards to pat her neck enthusiastically before turning back to where she could still see Jack and Buster watching her progress. She waved crazily, Jack waved back, and then they were gone from sight and there was just the sea, the clear sky and the awesome drop into the waves way below.

She wasn't sure at first where the sound came from. It started so quietly that it seemed to be the waves, swishing on the shore. The swishing turned into a crashing, the crashing of an angry sea upon the rocks, and her heart turned cold. Somehow she expected to hear the screaming neigh that echoed inside her head.

It came from the sea, was the sea... but no, it couldn't be. Magic reared, trying to wheel around, Grace grabbed for her mane, struggling with the reins and then, quite suddenly, the sound just faded. Magic stood stock still, head down and sides heaving while Grace still clung to

her neck with numb arms and a racing heart, waiting…
waiting for what?

The sea lapped gently against the rocks, a warm
breeze caressed her face and a million diamonds
sparkled upon the horizon. Was she going crazy? Magic
dropped her head, reaching for grass just as if nothing
had happened, and Grace picked up the reins, shivering
inside, not wanting to believe what she thought she had
heard. Nothing was going to spoil her perfect day.

"Come on, girl," she said, urging her into a sharp
canter. "Let's go home.

CHAPTER THIRTEEN

Despite her resolve to try to forget about her scare on the cliff top, Grace nevertheless checked and double-checked Magic's door before leaving her happily munching on a bulging net of haylage. There was no spirit horse, she was sure of it, but something had spooked her out there on the headland. Maybe it was the stallion again; maybe tonight it would try to come back.

She said as much to her mother as they ate their supper at the kitchen table. To her disappointment, her father would not be joining them tonight.

"I told you that it was early yet," Sue Melrose reminded her when she commented on his absence. "Anyway, what was it you were telling me about Magic?"

"Something spooked her again on the way home and I'm sure I heard a horse..."

"Look!" Her mother pushed her plate away and studied her daughter with a concerned frown. "I hope you aren't still worrying about spirit horses. I thought that we had resolved all that."

"We have," responded Grace determinedly. "I know that it was all my imagination, but there was a real horse, wasn't there? Maybe even a stallion. We both saw the marks on Magic's stable door so it must be real, but what if…?"

"What if what, hon?" asked Sue gently.

"What if it comes back?" blurted out Grace.

"Look," she reached across and covered her daughter's hand with hers. "I'm sure that whoever owns the horse will be keeping it much better supervised after it escaped before, but even if it does come back, then what do you think is going to happen? It couldn't get to Magic last time so there's no reason to believe that this time will be any different… not that there's going to be a 'this time,' of course."

"I know," sighed Grace. "And I realize that my imaginary spirit horse of the sea is totally crazy. It's just…"

"Just what?"

Grace stood up, scraping back her chair. "Oh, nothing," she said. "I'll just go and check on her one last time."

As she went to open the back door she stopped, looking back.

"She was awesome, wasn't she?"

Sue smiled, the soft sweet smile that Grace loved so much. "She was magic," she agreed.

Jack called at nine o clock. Grace almost told him about Magic misbehaving on the cliff top pathway, but thought better of it. To tell Jack would be to admit that she believed there was something to it and she wouldn't allow herself to think that.

"I thought I heard the stallion calling again on the way home," she eventually admitted.

"Then make sure the stable door is properly bolted," he insisted. "Just in case. You don't want your future champion to get stressed."

Grace put down the phone with a warm glow inside her. Jack had called Magic a champion. He was as confident in the filly as she. His words came back to her as she snuggled down in bed later that night and her mind drifted off into a future where silver cups and blue rosettes abounded.

She woke to see moonlight on her ceiling, silver lights and dark moving shadows. She pulled her comforter more tightly around her and closed her eyes again, shutting out the eerie shapes… and then she heard the sound. Was it the thud of unshod hooves or merely the wind blowing back Magic's top door?

The screaming whinny that rent the air seemed almost inevitable, and turned her blood icy cold. As she raced out onto the landing her mother appeared, eyes blurry with sleep and blonde hair tousled.

"What is it, hon?" she exclaimed, yawning. When the ringing neigh came again, there was no need for explanations.

"You were right," Sue breathed, already running down the stairs. "He's here! Quick, come on."

Outside the moon was so bright that Sue didn't even switch on the flashlight she had grabbed as they raced through the kitchen. Grace went first along the narrow pathway, bare feet cold on the concrete and bathrobe flapping behind her as she rounded the corner into the small stable yard. The sight she saw there stopped her in her tracks.

Magic's stable door stood open, hanging crookedly on one hinge, and a quick look into the gloomy interior simply proved Grace's worst fear. Magic was gone; her precious, wonderful horse was loose somewhere and possibly in danger. For a moment she froze, panic welling up inside her, taking away all conscious thoughts… *Where was she?!*

"Magic!" she screamed, "Magic!"

"Come on," called her mother. "I think I can hear them, out in the lane." Ahead of them the moonlight glistened eerily upon the sea and the melancholy moan of the wind echoed Grace's worst fears as it whipped over the cliff top. The trees on the headland were stunted black shapes, the lonely crash of waves against the rocks told of high tide.

"There she is," shouted Sue.

Two shapes appeared against the skyline, two horses standing close together, their necks entwined as if they were one being. Magic glistened silver in the moonlight and her darker, dappled companion, towered above her, his long mane lifting in the buffeting wind.

The breath left Grace's body as she moved slowly toward the cliff top. Her legs belonged to someone else, the whole world suspended in time as she waited for the inevitable… for history to repeat itself. And in the endless moment before her worst fears were realized the stallion raised his proud head and looked right at her, a mirror image of the painting on the stairs at Heathwaite Hall.

"Spirit," she breathed.

Her mother clutched her arm as he reared, flailing the air with his mighty hooves, and then they were racing, side by side, heads held high and nostrils flaring as they built up speed, across the meadow, faster and faster in a mindless gallop. Grace knew… long before they turned to charge back down the slope, she knew. The Spirit of the Sea had found his love at last, and he was taking her home.

One moment they were there, powerful and real, and then they were gone. He leaped from the cliff in one mighty bound and her precious Magic followed, disappearing over the yawning chasm and down, down, down into the raging sea. To Grace it seemed that her heart went too.

The next few days were a blur of pain, an empty place where she sat apart from the world. It had been inevitable from the start, she knew that now, and however much her parents tried to persuade her that the mighty stallion was real she knew the truth. She hadn't even been able to speak to Jack, or Nell. They both called again and again but her mother kept them away.

"No, not yet. Give her time…. She'll come around."

Grace knew that she would never come around.

Her father held out a ray of hope and the stable door stayed open, just in case.

"The tide was very high," he insisted. "And it was a fairly sheer part of the cliff, but there's still a chance that they may have managed to swim to safety… There's always a chance."

"But she would come home," cried Grace.

"There are miles of dense woodland along this coast. They may be hiding out somewhere, or maybe she's lost."

"Do you think that it's fair to get her hopes up?" chided Sue gently.

"You always have to have hope, love," he told her.

Hours turned into days, days to weeks and weeks at last to months; months of loss and loneliness. Grace roamed the shore for hours, searching… searching for what? Even she didn't know what she was looking for, except maybe a glimpse, some kind of proof that they really were gone. Still the stable door stayed open, tied back, welcoming.

Jack came over finally to find a very different companion than before. She looked the same, but her spark was gone and even he couldn't rekindle it. They walked together along the cliff top, retracing those agonizing steps again and again, searching for the daisy hooves, only to find them gone without a trace.

"Because it's over," Grace insisted. "The Spirit of The Sea has fulfilled his task."

"Don't be crazy," exclaimed Jack, but his eyes believed her.

Jack left in mid-summer.

"I'll be back," he promised, holding Grace's hand tightly in his. Then he gave her one quick hug and was gone. *Did everyone leave eventually?* she wondered.

Her father offered to buy her to a new horse to fill Magic's stable.

"It's the only way you'll get over it," he told her firmly. Grace imagined another face looking out over her silver filly's door and shook her head adamantly.

"That will be admitting that I believe she will never come back."

"Oh honey," said Sue. "You know it's too late for that."

At last it was time for school to start again and for the first time in her life Grace was looking forward to it. Life at home was a lonely place nowadays, and there at least she would have Nell to talk to; she had hardly seen her for the entire vacation.

She slipped into the routine with a kind of inevitability, but her teachers took her parents to one side and spoke of lowered performance and lack of effort. To Grace it was just survival, a waiting time.

"And that's the problem," murmured her father from behind the closed door of the living room. "Until she lets go and admits that Magic isn't going to come back, she'll never be able to get on with her life."

"Maybe she needs counseling," responded her mother in a worried tone and Grace turned away. *Did she need counseling? Was she going crazy?*

Nell said definitely not, but there was a worried look in her eyes. Oh, if only Jack would come back.

Every Saturday morning Grace re-did Magic's bed, straightening the banks into perfectly symmetrical shapes, refreshing her water bucket and redoing her hay net. Her parents watched with worried faces, but she just ignored them.

Even the magic of Christmas lost its cheer that year. Carefully chosen and deliberately non-horsey presents lay beneath the gaudy tree, still unopened by lunchtime. Grace knew that her parents were trying extra hard and that she was ungrateful and self-centered, but somehow she couldn't seem to snap out of it. She tried, she really tried, buying special gifts for both her parents and making a real effort to smile, but despite their delight she still felt as of she was in a private lonely place that hopes and dreams could not enter. Hopes and dreams had been the mainstay of her life just a few short months ago… but they had all included Magic.

It was on a cold and wintry morning toward the end of the winter break that she decided to go and see Mollie Jenkins. It had been Jack's idea, of course. He often e-mailed her with light-hearted observations about life in general. Maybe he *was* just trying to cheer her up, but it seemed to Grace in her own lonely world that she was the only one who remembered Magic now.

But then she realized that he had known all along, for instead of just e-mailing he called her, totally out of the blue one dreary Saturday afternoon. He whole body felt weak when she heard the sound of his voice and for the first time since he'd left, she looked out of the window and realized that the day wasn't gray and dreary at all. A pale yellow sun brought a glitter to the frosty ground, reminding her painfully of the diamonds that had sparkled upon the sea as she rode home from the show on the last normal day of her life.

"Guess what, Grace," he exclaimed. "I'm coming back to stay with my gran again this spring."

When she didn't respond with any enthusiasm, he sighed. "Look," he went on tentatively, choosing his words with care. "You have to snap out of this and get on with your life. I know how you feel; we all do, but…"

"My parents have been talking to you, haven't they?"

"They're worried about you, that's all… Look, why don't you go and see my gran? She knows about all kinds of stuff and there's something she wants to show you."

Suddenly that seemed to Grace like the best idea ever. "I might go tomorrow," she agreed. "And… thanks for calling."

"You're a friend," he said simply. "I just want to help."

Grace woke early on Sunday morning with a sense of purpose for the first time in over nine long months. Today she was going to see the one person who might understand. So why hadn't she gone before? The answer came at once… because she had been too steeped in her own misery to think of it.

"Going out, hon?"

She hadn't noticed the deep-seated worry in her mother's eyes before.

"Just for a walk."

"Take care."

Suddenly Grace rushed across the room to give her a hug, tears pressing the backs of her eyes. "I am so sorry for being such a pain all this time."

"Oh honey," Sue said, fighting to control the rush of emotion that choked her throat, "we've been so worried about you."

"And I've been so worried about Magic," Grace replied quietly.

"Life goes on though, you know, hon."

Grace knew that her mother was right. She had thought it herself so many times.

"It would," she explained, "if I just knew that she wasn't coming back, if I knew that she was dead."

"I think that it's time to believe that now."

Grace looked at her mother and smiled. "I really am trying," she said.

Half an hour later she walked slowly along the cliff top pathway. For months she had walked this way again and again, and along the shore itself, searching for anything that might tell of Magic's fate. Now she suddenly realized that it was Spirit she was looking for. Was *he* still here, the magnificent stallion that had taken away her whole life? Yet she couldn't blame him for that. After all, he had only been searching for his lost love.

She quickened her pace, her heart racing. Now that he had found her, what then? Did he no longer haunt the shores of Beachy Heights? Was he gone at last after all these years, finally able to find peace?

For a moment she stopped, right on the headland, staring out across the glittering sea. The icy wind turned her cheeks and fingers numb, bringing back sensations that were slowly thawing her heart. What a price she had paid for his freedom.

✳ ✳ ✳ ✳ ✳

Mollie was in the kitchen. She smiled a welcome and ushered Grace across to the stove.

"Now get yourself warmed up and I'll make you a hot drink," she insisted.

Grace thought that she looked older than before, her translucent skin drawn tightly across her cheekbones, but her twinkling eyes were so like Jack's that they brought a pain to her heart.

"I've called to speak to you these last months, but your parents said that you were better left alone, to forget about Heathwaite Hall and the legend of Spirit. Do you agree with them?"

"They think that they know best, but I'll never forget," Grace cried.

Mollie handed her a drink. "And now?" she asked quietly. "Now what do you believe?"

Grace took a sip of the sweet warming liquid. "I asked you that day, do you remember, about the legend, and you said that things like that didn't really happen. But I could tell by your face that you believed it, too. You told me to be careful, but I wasn't careful enough, was I?"

"Who knows," sighed Mollie. "What will be will be. I just know that when I was your age all I dreamed of was Spirit, the mighty stallion of the sea, searching for his lost love."

"And now?" Grace's whole face was alight as she listened for the wise old lady's answer.

"Now I have grown old and sensible with time. My dreams were pushed way into the back of my mind… until you came along with your stories."

"They weren't stories," insisted Grace.

Mollie bowed her white head. "I know… I know that you believed them but with old age there comes a kind of common sense."

"And now," repeated Grace. "Now do you believe me?"

"Come." Mollie stood up slowly, expecting Grace to follow her along the tall dark corridor and out into the grand space of the hallway.

Just as before the stallion stared down at them,

from where the stairs turned up onto the landing above, arched neck, flared nostrils, regal and majestic... and yet.

"He looks different," murmured Grace, "The same but somehow different."

Mollie placed a firm hand on her shoulder. "I knew that you would see it."

"He's softer," murmured Grace. "More..."

"At peace?" finished Mollie.

A sense of awe brought a tremble to Grace's limbs. "You *do* believe it," she whispered. "You really do believe in the Spirit of the Sea... but then where is Magic?"

"Now, that I don't know," she sighed. "But somehow..."

She drew Grace back toward the cozy warmth of the kitchen.

"Somehow I think that we will find out."

Grace went over their conversation again and again on the way home. Her footsteps were lighter and she felt a new sense of calm deep inside, as if she too had found a little of the stallion's inner peace.

She smiled at her mother, noting the relieved expression that passed between her parents.

"How was Mollie?" asked her dad, with feigned disinterest.

"She believes me," answered Grace simply.

"We all believe you, hon," said her mother. "It's just..."

"Don't worry," smiled Grace, meaning it. "Somehow I think that everything's going to be all right."

CHAPTER FOURTEEN

Eleven months and three days. Soon it would be a whole year since Heathwaite Magical Mist and Spirit, the mighty stallion of the sea, leaped from the cliff top. Spring was upon them, bringing new life to the world, and soon Jack would be back. Grace longed to talk to him, to walk the cliff tops again with Buster running on ahead, bracing themselves against the wind that blew in from the sparkling sea. She hadn't spoken to Mollie again, for there was no need; they both knew what they knew. And Grace was prepared to wait, even though she didn't know what she was waiting for.

Saturday dawned, clear and bright. She went through her weekend ritual, carefully sloping the shaving banks, replacing the dried out haylage net, scrubbing the water bucket and refilling it at the tap on the yard. *Tomorrow Jack would be here!* Her heart raced at the thought.

Moonlight cast a pale gleam through her bedroom window when she switched out the light. She lay in the silence, watching weird shadows race across the ceiling. Was that a horse she could see… a galloping horse? Suddenly her heart felt heavy, flooded by emotion, and she turned her face away from the light to bury it into the cool softness of her pillow.

She didn't know what it was that woke her. Was it the wind, or the soft thud of hooves? Was it a gentle whinny in the eerie half-light?

She slipped from her bed, wrapped herself in her bathrobe and padded down the wooden staircase with cold bare feet. She listened to the silence, a heavy pregnant silence that stifled the whispering voices inside her head.

The glow of the moon brought light into the night, paving the way for her footsteps along the narrow pathway that led to the stable. Her heart raced as the back door banged shut behind her, pounding against her rib cage like a trapped bird. Her feet moved automatically, along the side of the house.

Way, way out, against the eerie sky the sea glistened beyond the cliff top, the melody of the waves singing in her ears as they crashed against the rocks. She held her breath unknowingly, her body tense and rigid. The question screamed inside her head. Why…what was happening to her? And then, suddenly, she knew.

A gentle nicker floated toward her through the fresh spring night, low and vibrant. She quickened her steps, acutely aware of every tiny sound, as if her body was waking up from a very long sleep. The distant bleat of a lamb, the bark of a dog… a rhythmic chomping from the stable just ahead.

It was no surprise to see a pale shape in the moonlight from behind the open door, to hear Magic's gentle snort. Grace felt no fear, just a sense of inevitability.

"I knew that you'd come back," she whispered, pressing her cheek against the filly's soft dark nose.

The aroma of horse assailed her senses and for a moment she closed her eyes, trying to contain the elation that made her want to scream out loud. Magic blew softly through her nostrils, tossing her beautiful head… and then she heard another sound…

"Spirit?" Grace breathed his name. No, it couldn't be.

She flicked on the light, blinking in its sudden yellow glow, her eyes unable to decipher at first what she was seeing.

It lay quite still, trusting the world, staring up at her with great dark eyes, eyes that were so familiar; a tiny replica of the mighty stallion, Spirit.

Magic nuzzled its perfect form, looking around with pride, and Grace felt the tears she had been withholding for so long release themselves from their prison to run in rivers down her cheeks.

The stallion was gone, she already knew that, but where had Magic been? Wandering in the woods maybe, unable to find her way home, or in some mystical place that only released her when the foal was born. The truth of it would probably die with the legend of Spirit, the mighty stallion of the sea. His search was over, she knew

with no shadow of a doubt. His line lived on and now he could rest. Grace had seen it in his eyes that day at Heathwaite Hall. It was finally over.

She closed the door, sliding the bolt home, eager to go and wake her parents yet needing just a moment.

"Goodbye, Spirit," she murmured into the velvety sky.

No answer came and she expected none. The stallion may be gone but his heritage lived on at last in the tiny creature that stared up at her through his father's eyes.

The future beckoned enticingly.